Griqualand

G000138479

By Oliver Strong

ISBN: 978-0-9955188-9-6

Word Count: 52,720

Contents

Chapter One: Xhosa Flees

In times gone by a place existed, though absorbed by our modern world its name and geography persist today. A land nestled between the Drakensburg mountain range to the west, the Cape colony of the British to its south, northwards the Xhosa kingdom of Natal and beyond that the Zulu kingdom.

Its genesis, in the early 1800's, seeded by frequent Zulu raids and a Xhosa evacuation, a place named "Nomansland" was formed via lack of population; a desolate region where few survived its precarious placement between British desire, Xhosa indifference and Zulu ire.

Into this vacuum entered a disenfranchised tribe named the Griqua. Wanderers from as far as Cape Town, they'd trekked by foot and wagon for 2 years, eventually crossing the Drakensberg Mountains. Many died before reaching Nomansland, today their bones serve as ink upon dusty pages of an epic South African tragedy.

A distance of 700 miles as the crow flies yet on foot carrying family and possessions, a treacherous trek over desert and mountain with fortunate few reaching their intended destination.

First to arrive were a population of Griquas, later known by the moniker of "Cape Coloureds", mixed with Xhosa. Next followed the Afrikaans, moving in around 1872 when the city of Kokstad was founded by its namesake and leader of the Griqua tribe.

Originally invited into this area by the British Governor of the Cape Colony during the 1850's, the Griquas had finally found a home.

Then came the Boers, evicted from the Cape Colony due to a clampdown on slavery by the British Empire, selling up they settled in Griqualand East.

Each male Griqua residing in "Nomansland" or by its new designation "Griqualand East" was given permission to secure a 3,000 acre plot of land for himself.

Most sold their stake to white farmers relocating from the Cape Colony, squandering their money on cheap booze and expensive women.

One of these white farmers was a man you may be familiar with, or not, nevertheless you will come to know his name, Bastijn Klein Soepenberg.

A descendant of the first Europeans to settle these lands; turfed out of the Cape Colony he found refuge in Griqualand East, a land where he might own a farm and slaves to work it.

Soepenberg was a man of average height and stocky build, as his work required. He dressed in dusty clothes, a yellowed shirt with rolled cuffs. Leather trousers and thick boots with a crumpled leather hat providing shade for wandering rat like eyes to scan hot African horizon.

Resting in a wooden rocking chair, heels planted on porch gate, the blonde haired Dutchman observed as workers hauled tobacco back to the barn.

A large, lash wielding, Griqua guided slaves, keeping them in line with his authoritarian air. Upon meeting the aura of Soepenberg slaves increased pace.

The blonde Boer, (boer being a Dutch term for burgher), grinned as he rocked back and forth examining his cash crop whilst stuffing a pipe full of the same African shag. The pit of his wooden pipe crackled beneath burning match as Soepenberg puffed cold chestnut into life. Smoke signals rose into clear blue African sky informing enslaved of their master's scrutiny whilst performing his bidding, men and women who once freely populated this region, the San people, had been transformed into little more than slaves of Griquas and white men.

Upon arriving in Griqualand East both white Boers and Griquas required labour to till their land and harvest crops. Fortunately for them a few remained present in this land, a nomadic tribe found across the sub-continent of Africa.

Wandering wherever rain fell and wind did blow, the San people resemble Zulu in many respects, seeding their culture from east to west and north to south. Physically they are quite different, even to white eyes, for they bear a distinctive feature. The San's eyes are a crescent shape, suggesting an Asian heritage in this African blood line.

Griqualand San were unfortunate enough to find themselves caught in the perfect storm.

Zulu and Xhosa to the north, Basotho tribesmen to the west in a land known as the Basutoland, Basutoland is now the Kingdom of Lesotho, as of then it was a British protectorate and so formed part of the beast encapsulating Griqualand's western, southern and eastern border ... the Cape Colony, the land of the British, it's ruler and High Commissioner Sir Henry Barkly.

Sir Henry was an Englishman born in Highbury, Middlesex, a former member of the houses of parliament, yet after Robert Peel's overthrow he found himself lost. His opponents offered a life line, the governorship of British Guiana. After demonstrating great skill in managing Her Majesty's territory abroad he was moved on to Govern Jamaica then further across the globe, finding himself in the Cape Colony.

The northern kingdoms of Xhosa and Zulu were ruled by chiefs Kreli and Cetshwayo respectively. Both fierce rivals, Cetshwayo sent frequent raiding parties into his rival's territory creating an area of the Natal designated by both Kreli and Sir Henry as "Nomansland", today in 1875 "Griqualand East" was populated by Griquas and Boers, Boers who'd sold their real estate in the Cape Colony and using those finances they purchased land from Griquas at knockdown prices.

A landscape of beautiful green hills resting beneath blue sky populated by fluffy white clouds, this was fertile land, its soil rich and dark, providing plentiful crops each harvest.

Here Soepenberg was able to farm tobacco using slaves purchased at market in Griqualand's central city, "Kokstad".

Men and women of Xhosa and Malay descent also returned from fields to barns. Each laboured beneath a large sack of tobacco leaves on his or her back. A tall well-built Griqua named Jan Le Fleur marshalled slaves, keeping them in order, concentrating their duties lest he rebuke tardiness via sturdy lash, his constant partner in discipline.

Jan was not a slave but a Griqua employee. As workers retrieved tobacco to be stored inside barns, Jan approached his employer.

"Unjani?" stated Soepenberg, boots up on the porch while he rocked back puffing coarse African tobacco.

The pair spoke in a mixture of language, a delicatessen of communication selected from the African Cape's cafeteria.

Similar to a thick hearty pie assembled from left overs, the British call it bubble and squeak, in this region of Africa a fitting analogy would be "Bobotie". Today bobotie it is the national dish of South Africa, a sweet and spicy dish of curried mincemeat baked with fruit and a creamy egg based topping, left overs thrown together to formed a beloved dish.

And just as the English language is a melange of ingredients, so is the language of Afrikaans, the former, much the same as the latter, using Germanic languages as its base, employing Dutch as its principal layer.

Afrikaans, a language formed more than one hundred years ago when the Dutch East India Corporation, better recognised by the "VOC" symbol which stood for "Vereenigde Landsche Ge-Oktroyeerde Oostindische Compagnie", decided to set up a refreshment station on the southern cape of Africa.

In 1652 a settlement was established, providing supplies to ships traveling to and returning from the East; it prevented Dutch crews from succumbing to afflictions such as scurvy on the long voyage between Holland and the Far East.

Although the Dutch were only supposed to set up a refreshment station on the Cape, fertile soil and plentiful lands sparked greed within initial settlers.

Within four years they were at war with locals as the Khoi and San tried to drive the Dutch from their most arable lands.

Initially the Dutch imported slaves from East Asia but soon took to using captured Africans as farm labourers.

"Unjani?" said Soepenberg, or in today's English "what's up?"

Jan, a fellow tall as he was broad wiped his brow while adjusting leather hat similar to that worn in the Australian outback, "One of them got away, but he can't be far, I'll need a few men to run him down."

Soepenberg's rocking motion ceased, all fell calm but for whisps of smoke shifting aloft before being dragged away by afternoon breeze.

The blonde haired Boer rose to his feet, "Which way'd he go?"

"West, I reckon he's making for the Mzimvubu River."
The Mzimvubu River … when spoken in Xhosa but translated into English it means "The place of the hippopotamus". The Mzimvubu River is one of South Africa's most important rivers, starting in the Drakensberg mountain range it's 160 miles long and exits into the Indian Ocean.

The river provides farmland with fresh water and fishermen with abundant catches; if followed one might also find one's way out of Griqualand and into British territory where slavery had been abolished since the 1840's.

"Bring the shackles," stated the Boer as he stepped inside his farmhouse before drawing a rather obtuse blunderbuss from dark to light.

Jan nodded his head and swung toward the barn where he recruited three reliable farmhands, horses, whips and shackles.

Checking his weapon was loaded the Dutchman calmly strolled to the centre of his corral, better known as a kraal in this region of the world.

Slaves watched on, wondering as to whether their compatriot might attain freedom, and if so, perhaps that same path would open to them? For the white man does often say, "Fortune favours the bold," whereas in these parts natives are more likely to recite a local insight, "Indlela ibuza kwabaphambili," or in English, "The way forward is to ask from those who have been before." Perhaps a marriage of white man's courage and black man's wisdom would lead these unfortunates to freedom?

Soepenberg saddled up, pulling his steed by its reins until it neighed into compliance. Trusted farmhands, Griqua men paid a wage to marshal his workforce, saddled up, shotguns poking out on one side of their saddles, whips and chains hanging on the other.

"Get them locked in the barn," stated Soepenberg before digging his spurs and making for the Mzimvubu River while Jan kept an eye on contemplative labourers.

Riding through kraal gates and into fields Soepenberg's band headed west. The slave was on foot and much of the distance between here and the river was flat with little opportunity to hide oneself.

Hooves pounded dirt, kicking dust on horizon as an unfortunate man of Xhosa descent made for freedom, turning his head frequently if only to witness a thunder cloud of spite gain ground.

The river was many miles away and so desperate slave decided to turn north and hide within tobacco fields until evening's shroud might obscure his departure.

Soepenberg had a keen set of eyes and on this flat ground it was a simple calculation to make. The Boer's saddled band turned in an effort to cut off his flight into fields, Griqua horsemen following their master.

With pounding heart and drenched brow a young man in his twenties pushed onyx legs as hard as an adrenaline filled heart might allow. Unfortunately for him his constitution was poor competition against Soepenberg's stallion, and as a fox might be chased down by a pack of dogs, or a wounded wildebeest mercilessly pursued by a pride of hungry lions, he was met before dissolving within green tobacco.

Surrounded by neighing and rearing horse, vile men cracked whips about his body. The Xhosa slave was forced to project his arms forward, defending his face.

"Chain that kaffir up!" snapped a blonde Boer pointing the barrel of his blunderbuss toward absconded serf.

A farmhand moved in, horsewhip aloft.

"Not yet, leave that to later," ordered Soepenberg.

A panting Xhosa, wrists in chains entered kraal to wide eyed wonder of confined colleagues.

Soepenberg dismounted and addressed one of his farmhands, "You, bring me a rack and put it here."

The fellow got down, secured his horse and with a second workman returned carrying one of many racks employed to air-cure tobacco leaves.

The racks, usually kept inside a large barn where curing takes place, was brought into the middle of the kraal. A formerly free Xhosa was bound by arms and neck.

Soepenberg took a whip from one of the farmhands, ripped the man's shirt off and proceeded to lash skin from back.

The fellow screamed with each crack, farm slaves winced. Soepenberg pushed his arm in deeper, flexing a master's assertiveness, bringing to heel those who might consider an equally foolhardy future venture.

Slaves and staff stood in the kraal while sun touched horizon, illuminating the horror of a young man lashed until he passed out.

Once he'd collapsed, losing consciousness due to the horrific pain of rope cracking skin, farmhands untied his bonds permitting fellow workers escort groaning slave into one of their communal huts for a night's rest.

The rack remained in the courtyard, resting upon blood soaked earth, a dark taint smearing ground below, a reminder of what might occur should any captive rebel against their master's will.

Every morning a hideous smudge greeted his coerced compatriots on the way to and in late afternoon from the fields, for they were all owned by a single man holding certificates of registration upon which their mark was inked.

Bastijn Klein Soepenberg was a wretched man, cruelty a common thread in the tapestry of his life. In the 21st century, society might have blamed his parents but these were harder times, when both men and women were pressed to take accountability for their actions rather than cast blame onto an ancestor in hope of absolution.

These people had no nanny state to step in when times became hard, instead they were forced to endure, for the social order in this part of the world had fallen into place by happenstance rather than ordination; and by no means was that social order static, depending on who or what and where you were did dictate your place on the totem pole of life.

In the Orange Free State the Boer or white man occupied the top rung and the African the lowest, yet close by in KwaZulu, the Zulu or African occupied the upmost notch while the white man wallowed at the bottom.

In Griqualand East the coloured ran the show, each race and colour jostling for position. In fact you can say that this area of Africa is no different than any other in this respect, only in so much as the white man had introduced some extra tribes into an interesting bobotie of cultures, languages and colours.

And so, with juxtaposed ethnicities and allegiances rubbing up against one another, life was tough, grievances commonly led to violence, especially during times of drought for the most valuable resource at this time and perhaps anytime in Africa were grazing lands, water, labour and women. Added to that, this area of Africa, namely the Cape, was a strategic position for European trade, the entire premise for the white man settling this land.

Upon ownership of The Cape passing to the British many Boer's decided to leave rather than surrender slaves and so misery eventually moved through the Orange State and on to Griqualand East where men made best of a tenuous situation.

Soepenberg had enough money from selling his farm in the Cape Colony to buy a large holding here in Griqualand, however, life wasn't to be as simple as he'd assumed.

For despite having made the trek with his wife she'd fallen ill with cholera. Hannah, Soepenberg's wife, was 28 years of age. Having travelled all the way from Holland to the Cape Colony with her father she met Soepenberg, a young Boer farmer in his mid-thirties.

After making the trek from Cape Town to Griqualand East she'd contracted Cholera, a deadly disease with no known cure.

Cholera is spread due to the consumption of unsanitary drinking water and or food; facts of which people were unaware during this era, often dumping human waste into a river where those taking the trek to Griqualand stopped to drink.

Bacteria would infect the intestine and since humans were the only known host and symptoms appeared sometimes within 2 hours, there was often little warning as to its onset.

Soepenberg took his anger out on those around him, those who occupied the lowest rung of Griqualand's societal order. For despite doctors visiting every day to tend his Hannah there was nothing they could do. It would be decades before a legitimate vaccine were created in France. Until then, men and women would succumb in their thousands to this disease.

Soepenberg paid for treatment, Hannah was regularly administered opioids to ease her pain, each day her eyes sinking further within their skull, her skin turning a blueish purple hue as blood flow diminished. The common outcome ... once a patient has entered this stage ... is death.

It gnawed his soul night and day, often released in lashes of fury gracing a man's back, Soepenberg's ire antagonised frequently by the most token of misdemeanours.

That morning Kokstad's resident Doctor's entered the kraal in his buggy.

As slaves exited the barn with tools, Doctor Albronda stepped down, his assistant tied horse and buggy to a post.

Doctor Gerhard Albronda, a man in his 60's peered down to examine a bloodied patch of earth beneath similarly stained tobacco rack.

Dressed in light cloth suit with bowler hat, his thick grey brow lifted at the sight; thick mutton chop sideburns ran down his face to touch a chubby, rounded chin.

Albronda lifted his hat while a young man's groaning graced his ears, back bloodied by yesterday's lash. The slave was unable to join fellow workers and so engaged in light duties on the kraal.

"Don't you worry about him Doc, he'll get by," called Soepenberg from the main residence doorway.

The doctor's sullen eyes detached from morose Xhosa mien, "If any of your workers require attention, I would be willing ..."

"Those kaffir's don't need anything except food, water and six of the best when they play up," replied Soepenberg in his typically upstart attitude.

The Boer's inclination had been carefully cultivated over many years of arduous farm work until finally sprouting as a poisonous plant; much like the dumb cane plant, brought to the cape from other parts of the world it established roots here, known in this area of the world as the elephants ear or as the English say, "mother-in-law's tongue", due to its poisonous properties.

The Boers, originally from Europe had been transplanted into Africa bringing great wealth and becoming an integral part of the local genus, yet there was a poisonous aspect to their genetic makeup.

Doctor Albronda, a portly fellow of average height, lifted his medical bag from the buggy's rear as his Griqua assistant secured their single horse to a hitching post outside the house, "Your employees are only human Mr Soepenberg."

Soepenberg struck a match before bringing its crackle to wooden bowl and igniting a ball of African shag, "They're replaceable, Hannah isn't."

"I understand, but in all truth you should love those who sleep inside your huts during night and work your fields during the course of day as much as your own wife."

Soepenberg took a puff on his pipe and with a somewhat incredulous expression he replied to the doctor's rebuttal, "You what? Why should I care about a bunch of lazy blacks?"

Stepping onto the porch the doctor stood eye to eye with blonde haired Boer, "If you love those who love you, what credit is that to you? For even sinners love those who love them?"

"Bah, where'd you hear that rubbish?" spat Soepenberg plucking pipe from lips while smoke exited mouth.

"Your absence from church has not gone unnoticed this past year."

"Hannah's ill."

"All the more reason to attend," rebuked the doctor as he moved past a stunned Soepenberg and inside the main house.

The boorish Boer followed Doctor Albronda inside, puffing his pipe with indignation, "Puh, are you telling me Reverend Dower can perform miracle healings now?"

The Doctor halted inside a brick building with roof of wood and straw. Turning around he hitched a pious gaze upon Soepenberg, "Please extinguish your pipe, and if you don't mind, refrain from coarse remarks concerning the Reverend."

"This is my house you know!"

"Yes Mr Soepenberg and a clear atmosphere is conducive should there be any restoration in Hannah's health."

Soepenberg plucked pipe from lips and scrutinized its brown bowl, "I was told tobacco smoke disinfects the atmosphere."

"Really?" stated Doctor Albronda, "Pray tell, which physician made such a claim?"

"Nah, it was Jon."

"Jon?"

"Yeh Jon Visser ... the tobacconist."

Doctor Albronda snatched the pipe from Soepenberg's grasp, emptying its contents on the stone floor before stomping out smouldering embers, "On my return to Kokstad I shall have a word with Mr Visser, now, please lead me to Hannah."

Chapter Two: Hannah

Soepenberg entered a modest bed chamber occupied by his beleaguered wife, Hannah. She slept in silence. Even in this dim light her skin reflected an odd blue, almost purple tint, indicating her advanced condition. Glow from a nearby fireplace clashed with lilac inhabiting once fair cheeks.

A maid waited night and day on the lady of the house, keeping Hannah warm and plying her with hot drinks. Soepenberg began to stuff rough African shag inside brown pipe, its wood sourced from local chestnut. Doctor Albronda approached from behind and snapped under his breath, "I hope you do not intend on igniting that weed around my patient?"

"Why not?" protested Soepenberg.

"Shhh, reduce your tone sir!"

"Aye, alright doc."

"Tobacco is not to be consumed anywhere near your wife sir, it could be detrimental to any possibility of recovery." Soepenberg's gaze fell softly upon his Hannah, secluded under warm sheets which were changed for fresh linen every day.

Once vibrant chestnut eyes subdued beneath heavy lids and when exposed to light they seemed dull.

Her sickness reached within his soul, Hannah, the only thing he'd cared for in this world, the only thing that cared for him now lay night and day teetering on the boundary separating life from death.

A ship sailing the world's edge during an era when sailors believed it flat, and if one travelled too far in any one direction he might slide within an abyss, swallowed by a maelstrom that is the chaotic kingdom of Hades.

So his wife listed back and forth on the verge which discerns light from dark. Tilting into the gorge of hell, yet Hannah did divine Soepenberg's form, grasping her hand, calling her name, and so she careened from chasm and into light.

Hannah's malady afflicted her husband with an anxiety he'd not experienced before now, a terrible frustration born of observing his wife's precarious journey, teetering on the threshold marking God's doorway to the kingdom from which none return.

For a moment Soepenberg was transfixed, scrutinizing his wife as she groaned on the outskirts of existence.

Doctor Albronda moved past the blonde Boer to Hannah's bedside, the maid pulled up a stool and smiled as he placed his medical bag on the floor, "Would you like a drink Doctor?"

"What have you been providing Hannah?"

"Tea doctor, good and strong."

"Excellent, I'll have the same please."

"Yes doctor," replied the maid before leaving Doctor Albronda to his work.

Albronda delicately grasped Hannah by her wrist while removing a pocket watch from his waist coat, "Have you been keeping house fires lit at night?"

"Aye, and it's damn uncomfortable!" replied Soepenberg, inserting his pipe inside a dusty old jacket.

It was late summer in Griqualand and the climate remained somewhat warm, for harvesting tobacco was not a one and done deal but a perpetual activity, every 2-3 weeks leaves are harvested from fields and set aside for curing.

Albronda raised a bushy grey eyebrow switching his vision to the Boer for a moment, "Fires must be kept up, your wife is most vulnerable to an attack at night. Warmth chases out not just cold but damp, another of Hannah's enemies."

Soepenberg said nothing as the doctor's attention returned to his patient.

"Yet avoid exposure to extremes, heat included."

"Aye doc."

Cholera was a terrible affliction of the 19th century; originating from a pandemic in 1816, in India. Via trade routes it was spread across the globe, killing millions, rich and poor, from lowest beggar to King Charles X of France and the American President James K. Polk.

Maintaining warmth and personal cleanliness were of utmost importance, in both prevention and treatment of this century's scourge, and exposure to damp to be avoided.

Warmth, dryness and regular ventilation was Doctor Albronda's mantra.

The maid returned with warm tea, Soepenberg moved a bedside table setting it neatly beside the doctor, permitting his workbag space, besides the tea.

"Thank you," said the doctor, placing instruments of his trade atop chestnut table.

Doctor Albronda was a general practitioner ... and a rural practitioner such as he did lend himself to many aspects of a physician's work. From setting limbs to pulling teeth to treating diseases such as cholera; physicians of this age rarely specialized, except for those practicing within large metropolitan areas.

Travelling via buggy or even canoe, Doctor Albronda's work bag was made of tough leather, designed to carry everything he might require upon meeting his destination while keeping those tools safe and dry, much like Hannah.

Albronda produced a glass thermometer, a recent addition to his armoury since these objects only began to appear in the civilized world in the 1860's.

Gerhard had acquired one while shopping for new equipment in Cape Town, removing the glass stick from his tool bag and placing it beside a bottle of antiseptic.

"What's that?" inquired the blonde Boer leaning over Albronda.

"A thermometer Mr Soepenberg, it's used for taking a patient's temperature."

"I know that, I mean that bottle!"

"Please lower your tone."

The Boer quietened down as his wife groaned while shifting around the bed, her tawny brown hair spread across fluffy white pillow.

"This bottle contains a high concentration of spirits."

"Spirits?" whispered Soepenberg, "You said she ain't supposed to drink."

"It is not for consumption but to rub upon her skin, as an antiseptic."

"How's that going to stop her getting sepsis?"

"Despite beliefs upheld in the new world, germs do not spontaneously generate themselves. I have studied Mr Pasteur's theories and find them quite sound.

I believe that before evening sets in, should you rub this on Hannah's skin it will discourage germs from attacking her body."

It was not just the new world that disagreed on the origins of germs; there was much debate amongst the medical community on all continents.

Soepenberg merely scratched his head as Doctor Albronda executed his trade.

In city slums all along trade routes connected to India, cholera did rage. Here in Griqualand there was much open space, yet unfortunately, it is believed Hannah contracted her condition doing voluntary work for the church in Kokstad.

It was for this reason Soepenberg came to hate blacks, blaming them for his wife's predicament, and so his reputation grew as the hardest slave master in this locality.

As Hannah groaned under her malady so slaves heaved beneath their own plight, for should they incur the slightest infraction Soepenberg did dispense the whip, not only in correction but retribution for his afflicted Hannah.

Ironically, the very reason he'd made the trek of tears to Griqualand (so he may own other human beings as property) had ended in Hannah's infirmity. Yet Soepenberg blamed those he enslaved for his wife's misfortune.

"Hmm, I do believe the rains are coming next month, is that not correct Mr Soepenberg?"

"Aye, but you never know in this cursed place."

"Well, be prepared to keep your entire property drained, a dry environment is crucial to Hannah's recovery."

"Aye, I've got ya. When they've brought the crops in I'll have them dig drainage ditches."

Doctor Albronda brushed a dry cloth on Hannah's milk white forehead, "Hannah," he whispered in a delicate tone, "Hannah, do you hear me?"

Her tired vision creaked open to reveal once vibrant cinnamon eyes, today they were dull, glazed by a hell that is cholera. Hannah made a small smile.

"Hey! She notices you!" yelped Soepenberg.

Albronda sprained in Soepenberg's direction delivering a furious visage, to which the blonde Boer fell mute, "Sorry doc," he whispered.

The excitement at seeing his wife awake and perhaps notice an old friend had been too much to hold back.

"Hannah," continued the doctor, stroking teal brow, "are you there?"

Hannah, her body for the most part hidden beneath thick bed linen, gave a weak nod.

"Do you recognise me?"

Hannah lifted a delicate hand resting on top of the sheets and the doctor quickly moved to grasp it, lest her pasty palm peel away, void of life.

Her hand was cold and clammy, "Do you recognise me Hannah?"

Her petite cobalt mouth opened as a drawbridge might slowly extend, "Doctor?"

"Yes Hannah, Doctor who?"

She forced the words as her husband might drive a band of tired slaves into fields on a morning, "Albronda?"

The doctor smiled, "Yes, that's right Hannah, Doctor Albronda. You're looking better Hannah."

She shook her chestnut bonnet with much effort from left to right.

"Now, now Hannah, we mustn't think like that, I'm telling you that your health is looking up, why you'll be about in a month or so."

The auburn haired lady, her skin tainted by deadly disease, made a groaning noise from deep down as weighty eyelids fell, closing as a window shutter in an inn at chucking out time, her head turned and she fell beneath the spell of Hypnos.

Floating in and out of the Greek god's daze Hannah had managed to avoid his grasp, for but a moment, before he dragged her back to the underworld while his twin brother, Thanatos, orbited as a dark beast, waiting to take her into the domain from which no man, save Odysseus, has ever returned.

"Hannah," whispered Gerhard, holding her hand by the palm whilst lightly tapping the back, "Hannah, are you there?"

"Doctor, she won't wake again, not until afternoon," stated the black maid.

"I see," replied Gerhard, "How often does she wake during the day?"

"In the morning, afternoon, and sometimes before evening sets in; she's awake for no more than ten minutes at a time, until her cramps have passed."

Doctor Albronda set Hannah's delicate hand on the bed, "I see, do you change her under-garments?"

"Yes Doctor."

"And?"

"Lady Hannah has no control of her bowels doctor."

The Doctor placed his long thermometer in Hannah's armpit whilst checking her chest with his stethoscope, shifting it place to place, first locating an echo on her heartbeat then monitoring her lungs, "Well done Aunty, how often is the linen changed?"

"Every day Doctor, and I have the staff expose it to sunlight, her food is clean, no fruit, no cold, only hot stew and warm milk sir."

Gerhard nodded his head as he removed his stethoscope before pouring himself a cup of tea, added a drop of milk then took a sip.

"Well doc?" inquired Soepenberg beneath his breath. Gerhard merely took another sip of warm tea before packing away his utensils. Albronda snatched one last reticent glance at Hannah before rising from wooden stool, "Outside if you please."

One of the remedies for treating cholera, in that age and ours, is to make certain that every cause tending to depress the moral and physical energies of the afflicted be averted.

Doctor Albronda didn't want to discuss Hannah's condition or her chances of pulling through within earshot. She may be unconscious … seemingly … but who knows? Hannah may wake and in her delirium eves drop on the solemnity of her situation, leading to a depressed state of mind.

The pair exited, bequeathing responsibility of the lady of the house back to Aunty.

In an adjacent room Doctor Albronda's visage became the image of sincere sobriety, sending a chill of terror through Soepenberg's body … similar to a young man at his wedding … future thoughts clashed with one another in Soepenberg's mind, causing his frame to shake as a tree blasted by hurricane force winds.

"Your wife has been captured in the throes of this terrible disease for some time sir. She is too ill to move to Kokstad and I'm afraid there is little else I can do but pay regular visits.

Her fate rests firmly in the hands of God now. I suggest you have Reverend Dower visit as soon as possible."

"What?" Soepenberg raised his voice, "Why would I have 'im on my property? He cares more for those damn blacks than decent folk!"

"Sir, lower your tone so as not to disturb Hannah."

"Sorry doc."

"And as for the Reverend he serves all of God's creatures. I suggest you invite him here as soon as possible, Hannah's remaining time may be scant."

"What do you mean?"

"I mean to say, if the Lord is willing to make a difference you should employ the Reverend forthwith ... before it is too late. You don't wish to neglect the exploration of every avenue only to suffer the regret of inaction should your wife pass."

Soepenberg's bright blue eyes sparkled with fear, the doctor wasn't playing games, he'd obviously reached the same conclusion as Soepenberg ... Hannah's life hung in the balance, "Aye, I'll go to Kokstad and have a talk with 'im."

"I suggest you do more than that sir, I suggest you beseech his presence immediately, Hannah cannot wait."

Soepenberg nodded his head, "Aye, I'll do that today."

The doctor made his way out and back to the buggy, "Unfortunately there's little we can do now but pray, Hannah's fate is truly in God's hands."

"Aye, well I never had much in the way of faith," replied a downtrodden Boer.

As the doctor reached his buggy he placed medical bag on the rear seat, nodded to his assistant who unhitched the ride and prepared for their journey to the next farm.

Before stepping up and in, the doctor's vision locked with that of Soepenberg, "Then I suggest you find it sir, for Hannah's sake. I have witnessed faith do much in the way of recovery especially concerning cholera, never discount it."

The doctor lifted his leg, rested his right foot on a step and climbed into the buggy, "Faith Mr Soepenberg is a great healer, miraculous even."

"Aye, thanks doc, I'll see you next week?"

"Provided weather permits, and don't forget the spirits, I've found them to be a wonderful anti-septic, goodbye."

Albronda's assistant tapped their horse and exited the kraal, leaving Soepenberg alone. For a few moments his mind was distant before gathering his thoughts and shifting toward a hut his Griqua staff occupied, "Aye! Jan! You there?"

"Yes boss?" stated a tall coloured man, in his 30's, well-built and good looking.

"Get the wagon ready, we're going into town, I've got business."

"Aye boss."

Jan began to prepare the wagon, while doing so the tall Griqua noted to his employer, "Boss, we need mortar and some supplies for the workers."

"What supplies?" inquired Soepenberg.

While trapped in orbit of his wife the Boer's mind had lapsed concerning the state of his labourers.

"We need some biltong, boss."

"I bought a load of supplies last week, they can't have gone through it already?"

"That was the Malays, the Sans won't eat their bunny chow."

Just to clarify, biltong is a cured meat lightly flavoured with spice whereas bunny chow is a Malay dish, very popular in South Africa today, served to workers. It consists of a hollowed out loaf of bread, think of a large burger bun. Inside is filled with spicy Malay curry, a labourer would carry it with them into the fields or wherever they work, it served as a convenient method of storing your lunch.

Today it is sold as street food originating on the Eastern Cape of South Africa, brought in by immigrant slaves from India and Malaysia; it is now a mainstay of the country.

Bunny chow agreed with slaves from the East yet purebred African palates were unimpressed.

"Pah! They can have bobotie or starve!" snapped Soepenberg.

"Boss, they can't go out without a full belly, you know that."

Jan was right, despite his desire to cast their request aside, tobacco farming, up until the 1950's, was a very labour intensive endeavour.

On average it took 900 man hours to cultivate just one acre of tobacco and Soepenberg's farm had 200 hectares, or 500 acres, of arable land.

It meant that a lot of land had to be worked by as many slaves as possible, and they weren't going to harvest his crop while bellies clung to backbones.

Soepenberg looked up to the sky, weather was changing and autumn would be setting in. Here in Griqualand autumn, then winter brought with it hail storms, floods and powerful winds, he couldn't risk it.

The more ruthless the breed of Boer the more likely he was to make the mistake of harvesting crops late. Then there was the other expression of ferocious farmer, deliberately retaining tobacco in its curing barn so as to find higher prices at market, once demand exhausted initial yields.

Many of those men were punished by Mother Nature for such daring. Watching their profits collapse along with the barn in which it'd matured, returns cast to the winds by hurricane force currents, revenue washed away on the delta of Mother Nature's retribution.

Soepenberg, despite his greed, was cautious during these days, "Alright, bring one of the San, she'll know what to get."

"Aye boss," Jan made for a large hut housing the San.

Slaves in this region were divided into three main groups, San, Xhosa and Malay and kept separate from one another; they didn't get along due to disputes not only culinary but cultural.

For reasons the white man finds difficult to understand they didn't trust one another.

Yet Soepenberg, having picked up the language of Afrikaans was able to communicate with the San and so understood their distrust.

Why, he trusted none of them either but he felt more comfortable around San.

The look, the smell and the fact Malay often communicated in a language totally foreign to both black and white unsettled Soepenberg. All of these factors culminated in heightened distrust of Asian slaves.

Everything about the San meshed favourably with Soepenberg's sensibilities. The language for example; Afrikaans was a language of contact formed when Dutch and Africans, known as the Khoisan, met on the Cape. A common form of communication between white and black tribes, it was founded in the mid-17th century and developed from there.

Known as Cape Dutch for the longest time, it was influenced by Khoisan slaves speaking a form of pidgin Dutch. Overtime Afrikaans circulated while it morphed, considered beneath official Dutch, men such as Soepenberg spoke it fluently, out of necessity.

Eventually, in the 20th century, Afrikaans replaced standard Dutch as the Dutch language in South Africa. Previously considered 'kitchen Dutch' or 'bastard jargon' it was looked down upon.

It is a fact in the development of Afrikaans that from 1652 – 1672, at least 75% of the children born to slaves in the colony had white fathers. Picking up the Dutch language and speaking it imperfectly was a major influence on the language of Cape Dutch.

Jan appeared from the San huts, separating San from Malay slaves. Behind him followed a tall San, taller than Soepenberg, a full five feet and ten inches.

The San, one of two tribes to meet the Dutch on the Cape, the other being the Khoi, were particularly prized; their ability to learn and communicate in multiple languages a factor in their higher price at market.

They'd co-habited with the Dutch since first contact and so were selected as house slaves. A familiarity between white Dutch and black Khoisan led to a closer relationship not only concerning slaves but between members of their own community, for men such as Soepenberg knew many San by name.

Jan walked up to his employer, "Alright boss, Arnou's coming with us."

Soepenberg set his eyes on the tall woman, a slim frame attached to a set of muscular legs. Despite her status she stood proud, as an eagle in her roost, surveying savannah below with an eye to inflict mayhem upon any creature crossing her sensibilities.

Chapter Three: Kokstad

Arnou's lanky frame glistened beneath African sun, a regal figure adorned in a brown animal skin crossing her chest, looping a long neck.
A recently shaved head reflected morning sun, Soepenberg found her visage disquietingly noble, for despite a lowly position in life she refused to walk with head low.
Arnou's mid-riff was exposed, offering a slick of perfectly proportioned melanin deep in both pitch and wonder.
Her hips hugged by faded skin from the same beast ended above her knees; guarding her feet a pair of sandals constructed of the same material, protecting this proud creature from daytime heat of African sun gracing earth to such intensity it would scorch the underside of a man's foot.
A once dignified member of the San tribe, she was captured in a Zulu raid on Nomansland. Her fiery attitude memorialised upon her back in the form of many wounds, not from the white man but Zulu and Xhosa alike.
Her people were a nomadic tribe caught in a titanic tussle for power on this continent's Eastern Cape.
White fought white, and black fought black, in between coloureds took sides amid white factions.
On the east of the cape, amongst the white man, Dutch and British were in conflict; by increments the lion gained an upper hand.

Amongst natives, Zulu were in dispute with Xhosa, Zulu in ascendance.

Khoisan trapped amidst all, their best hope was in fact the British, for they were the only abolitionists on the face of the planet. It was their policy, wherever located, to free slaves and if a nation's policy were in contradiction, then a pretext for all-out war had been justified.

In the name of God, Queen Victoria and all that was right they did often administer brutal redress upon scoundrels who might flout all that is decent and honourable in the world.

The British upper class saw themselves as enforcers of honour and civilization in a world of miscreants and barbarians.

Arnou had been the victim of Zulu raids into the Natal region. Captured and forced into work she was beaten on a daily basis, cuts to her face failed to obscure her beauty.

Once sold to white men she was taken to market in the Orange Free State, a country founded by Boer farmers just north of the Cape Colony.

Purchased by Soepenberg, who'd recently set up a farm with his wife Hannah, she was given the position of house servant, essentially a house slave.

Arnou's ability to communicate and the fact the San people were familiar both with and to whites originating from Holland made her a perfect fit for this position.

Then came the British, exerting their rule, turning the state into a protectorate, forcing the emancipation of slaves.

Many Boers sold up, moving on rather than pay farmhands a wage. Some struck north for the Transvaal Republic, others east for Griqualand East, founded by a coloured gentleman, Adam Kok III.

Here in Griqualand Soepenberg purchased a farm from one of many Griquas who, after being given permission to sequester a plot by the administration, decided to cash in for quick money.

Today Arnou worked the house, cleaning, cooking and serving her master's needs.

Arnou stepped past a bloodied tobacco rack in the centre of the yard, a form of punishment familiar within Zululand. Beneath that barren perch of wood a stretch of brown stained earth resided in remembrance of what was in store for any slave who dared flee Bastijn Klein Soepenberg.

"Aye, Arnou, stop gawping and get up here!" called the blonde Boer pulling her attention from a trestle of torment.

"Yes Master," replied dutiful slave, walking to the opposite side of the wagon and getting in before Jan. She sat between the pair, Soepenberg dressed in thick cotton work shirt, shifted the brim of his outback hat upwards and looked her in the eye, "Don't you worry about him, I've not killed a slave yet," he looked forward and tapped a set of reins on the horse's back, "not one of my own anyway."

Arnou was momentarily concerned yet soothed herself upon recalling the special value a San slave held at auction, looking forward she remained silent as they journeyed for an hour into Kokstad.

Kokstad was the capital city of Griqualand East, named after Adam Kok III, its founder and current ruler of this state.
Rather than rule as a feudal king he led in a more civilized fashion, somewhere between his neighbours, a blend of black and white, much like the Griquas themselves.
He headed a full counsel of individuals who acted sometimes as ministers, sometimes advisors, often both, and it was he who both the British governor of the Cape Colony and Kreli the Xhosa King would deal with.
As for King Cetshwayo of the Zulu, he considered himself too powerful to be worried with border politics ... and he was correct.
The Impi were sent wherever he pleased, if he wished to raid Griqualand he did so and no-one was able to stop him.
For Griqualand occupied an area evacuated by Kreli due to frequent Impi incursions.

In 1820 the Griqua tribe, founded by a descendant of Adam Kok III, lived in Griquatown in the Cape Colony.
They first settled in Philippolis, north of the Cape Colony in the Orange River Free State; Philippolis having been founded by the London Missionary Society in 1823 to serve the local Griqua people.

First there was conflict between the San and Griqua people, with Griquas using Philippolis as a base of enterprise to run guerrilla warfare operations ... the San were pushed away.

Naturally, karma decided to make an appearance sinking her long teeth into Griqua flesh. Voortrekkers, essentially Boers who'd fled the Cape Colony to escape British law concerning the abolition of slavery, made their way to the Orange River Free State.

Tensions grew between mixed raced Griquas and Dutch descendants, a compromise was met, Adam Kok III permitted Boers take out long leases on Griqua farmland, Soepenberg being amongst their number. Yet when those leases were up and Griquas desired their land back, Boers refused to hand it over and violence broke out.

So in 1861 Adam Kok III accepted a British offer to travel over the Drakensberg Mountains and settle an area know as "Nomansland".

So the Griqua tribe took it upon themselves and made a two year trek from Philippolis to Griqualand East. Most of their cattle died alongside many of their tribe, journeying over the Drakensberg Mountain range.

Years later Soepenberg did follow them, for the British moved in, forcing protectorate status upon the Orange River Free State and abolishing slavery.

Griquas from whom he'd stolen had their revenge, be it from the grave.

And so Soepenberg and Arnou both hated Griquas, something which united them, making Jan the odd man out in this multi-coloured threesome entering the town ok Kokstad.

Kokstad was founded on the outer slopes of the Drakensberg Mountain range, 4,000 feet above sea level. Behind the town Mount Currie rises to a height of over 7,000 feet.

That was in 1861, in 1869 Adam Kok requested that Reverend William Dower settle a mission in Kokstad. He agreed to do so on the condition the Griquas move their settlement to a more agreeable location, on the Mzimhlava river (a tributary of the Mzimvubu river).

So Kokstad moved to its new location with Europeans playing major roles in its development, most prominent being two Scottish gentlemen George Brisley and Donald Strachan who established Kokstad's first major trading store, Strachan&Co.

They introduced the first indigenous currency to South Africa, a set of trade tokens manufactured in Germany and circulating over an area as large as the country of Ireland.

Today was 1875, the town had flourished and Griqualand was doing well for itself, yet the imperial lion's belly rumbled once more. After satisfying its appetite upon the Orange River Free State the beast looked toward his next meal and despite being but a morsel Griqualand would satisfy its yearning, for a short while.

And so this was the subject of discussion when Soepenberg entered the Town Hall. Adam Kok III stood before a mix of Griquas and Boers while explaining their tenuous situation.

Soepenberg rarely attended such events, he believed politics to be superfluous to his business, despite his past. Yet today solemnity lay thick on atmosphere as fertilizer upon field, encouraging shoots of strife to break fertile African ground and bask beneath British sunlight.

"I have it on good authority the new Governor Henry Bartle is not only replacing Sir Henry Barkly but his General is to be replaced with a man named Chelmsford. This news could be detrimental for every hard working man in Griqualand.

I have called this council to decide our course of action when General Chelmsford arrives."

Soepenberg quietly listened, stuffing his pipe with rough African shag while scrutinizing a tall coloured gentleman at the podium, mutton chop sideburns touching his lower jaw. Adam Kok III was dressed in a suit with waistcoat and cravat, a square of white silk falling into his waistcoat, worn on the outside of a small collared, white shirt. He might have been confused for the new governor himself, were it not for his mixed heritage, a cape coloured.

Adam's unique Cape accent, a mix of the Afrikaans and Khoi not only betrayed his bloodlines but seated this sable statesman further from his white contemporaries.

The Griquas Khoi heritage is why said tribe rubbed Sans the wrong way, for the Khoisan are not a single tribe but two. Only in this area of Africa are the two shelved in the same pigeon hole, an oversight leading the ignorant to mistake them for a single entity or at least friendly to one another, this is a falsehood.

A young Boer dressed much the same as Soepenberg, a typical fashion to bushman of that era, raised a fist as he declared, "We can fight!"

A noise of approval, from younger men, clashed with grumbles of disdain exiting elders.

"What? Are you afraid of the British?" he said in an Afrikaans tone.

No man was willing to grasp the gauntlet he'd thrown down, through shame, fear, or just waiting on a lion to lead these sheep.

Soepenberg looked around the room and realised should no-one speak Adam Kok would discount the option of self-defence in short order.

Deciding to add his voice to that of the young bushman Soepenberg took a puff on his pipe before plucking it from betwixt lips, "Aye, if we don't stop 'em, they'll come here like everywhere else and steal our slaves."

An elder gentleman in his late fifties sitting at the front of the hall turned around and rebutted Soepenberg, "Steal? I got a decent price for my slaves when they took the Free State."

"Aye, half of what you paid, if you're lucky, some of us got nothing!" snapped a bitter Boer sitting close by.

Soepenberg smiled inside, his argument was gaining traction. Outwardly he maintained a hardened visage, as a judge presiding in the Crown Court on a case most foul in nature, "Aye! I was robbed by them flapdoodle bastards!"

(A "flapdoodle", in this context, would equate to something like "limp dick" today).

Adam Kok ventured to speak as loud muttering travelled the hall, "Gentlemen! Enough of that language! We are here to consider our options and reach a decisive course of action, not throw insults at approaching fate,"

"We can organize a militia, that might be enough to put them off," submitted the blonde tobacco farmer.

"Mr Soepenberg, as it stands we have neither funds nor men required to give the British army cause for concern, unless you have a suggestion as to how we might counter that quandary?" replied Kok.

"We can raise a tax," replied the blonde Boer.

A heightened discord of disapproval overtook the room as waves battering cliffs with turbulent salt water echoing from one stone wall to its opposite.

Kok gripped a gavel, firmly striking the desk before him until their salty swell died, "Very well," his eyes fixed on Soepenberg, "tell me Mr Soepenberg, to what extent would you be willing to finance this venture?"

Everyone fell silent, vision locked on Soepenberg as hyena during night, ears pricked intently.

The Boer's eyes narrowed on Kok, he realised what he'd done yet he was obliged to reply, "Well it's not been the best harvest and most of my tobacco is still curing in me barn ..."

There was uproar amongst not only his Boer compatriots but Griqua farmers.

Kok slammed gavel against podium once more until thunderous cliffs subsided, "I see Mr Soepenberg, what about manning the militia? If you cannot donate coin, ought you not donate time?"

"Aye ... I can't do that," the blonde Boer betrayed his true nature, a white rat that when exposed to truth's light did scurry for the darkest tunnel he might find, "I've got a farm to look after."

"Then perhaps you might donate some of your slaves?" pressed Kok in an impetuous tone.

"I would, but I need them to turn a profit."

"Then pray tell sir, what exactly are you disposed to contribute in the name of our efforts?"

The white rat thought for a moment, "I can provide a ration of tobacco?"

A Griqua laughed, a sardonic laugh, "Pah! And he says the British are flapdoodles!"

There was raucous laughter, Soepenberg zeroed in and sneered, "You watch your mouth scrub!"

The Griqua took to his feet, a tall man over six feet with broad chest, an intimidating fellow by any standards, "Let's take this outside and see who's a scrub!"

Men became rowdy once more, for a short time this meeting may have resided within a pub, violence threatening to erupt at any moment. Adam Kok III looked on, he understood Griqualand East was incapable of levying a militia to stave off British incursion, yet he wished to make it plain before Griqualand's community, "Gentlemen!" Adam banged the gavel with rapidity mimicking that of a gatling gun, "how might we resist British encroachment when preoccupied with subjugating one another?"

Before the Griqua took his seat he growled at the white rat, "Another time Soepenberg."

"I'll be waiting scrub," snarled Soepenberg.

Adam Kok waited for the room's attention to rebound upon him. He gazed upon his audience before making his intentions clear, "I have discussed the issue at hand with my ministers and concluded armed resistance is out of the question. The Orange River Free State has been eyeing our land as have the Xhosa and we are too weak to repel a concerted effort by either.

Therefore … in compromise I plan to seek protectorate status from the British, solving all of our problems in a single document."

Uproar choked the room, as a thick smoke billowing from white and coloured chimneys alike, for both Griqua and Boer had sizeable investments in slave labour.

Adam's gavel slapped his podium with rapidity once more, "Gentlemen!"

Yet the crowd refused to yield, like a crash of rhino charging across dusty East African plains, their clamour frightened horses hitched outside Kokstad's town hall.

Adam persisted until this crash of Griqua and Boer eventually came to order, resting upon a river bank to bathe in cool brown mud.

"I commiserate with your hesitation gentlemen, many of you already having been forced into exile by the British and their abolitionist stance.

Yet I put it forth that I shall do my utmost to carve out an oasis where you may farm your land while maintaining slaves, outside the scorching eye of British legalise," announced Kok in an uplifting tone.

Some of the rhino, black and white, took nourishment from the fodder in his words yet Soepenberg was amongst those remaining unimpressed, "They tried that in the Free State but we had to move on."

"Mr Soepenberg, no-one is preventing you from unburdening your farm upon the open market, I'm sure you'll find a patron ... perhaps a Boer?" sniped Kok, a veiled reference to Boers purchasing land from Griquas who should've known better.

"Sell me farm? I'd barely get half of what it's worth now! Besides, I can't move my wife, she has to stay in bed all day, you know that."

"Mr Soepenberg, I have called this meeting of land owners to solicit solutions not confabulate complications. If you have a suggestion other than those proposed we are all listening."

The white rat thought for a few minutes, pulled a box of matches from his shirt pocket, struck a red headed stick on his boot and rekindled pipe.

He held the attention of every man of importance in Griqualand and was unlikely to do so again, so he put forth a further proposition, "Alright, how about we have a whip round and bribe the governor?"

Adam Kok's dark eyebrows shifted aloft, a dermatological disturbance ascended causing his brow to fold in several places constituting an odd pattern, much like a character in Japanese script, "Bribery Mr Soepenberg?"

"Aye, bribery, one thing I've learned over the years is that every man has his price," declared the rat, much to the agreement of several farmers, though not all were comfortable with such a thesis, perhaps they disagreed or were attempting to obscure their own villainous nature? Who knows?

Adam Kok looked down from podium as pastor from lectern, his vision filled with disdain as it scanned a mixture of utter ruthlessness and pure cowardice resting before him.

Here was a man, willing to do whatever it took to protect his family and property save that of putting his own mortality between them and the wickedness soon to descend upon the Griqua people once more.

No, Soepenberg would rather scurry away as a rat into its foul hole, sending other men to their fates, men who despite being coloured farmers still lived by a code of honour when it came to protecting what's theirs.

"Bribe a British High Commissioner? Are you sure Mr Soepenberg?"

"Aye I'm sure, I bet he can be bought just like every man here!"

The cliffs of honour began to thunder once more as the sound of Soepenberg's accusations broke against every bluff in the room.

"Ah, don't play coy with me, I know you lot, you'd whip your own mothers if it meant harvest came in a month sooner!"

Waves smashed against white chalk and brown granite, foamed spray repelling fiendish sea.

Adam's gavel struck its podium and men quietened down, "Mr Soepenberg, a British High Commissioner is above reproach unless you can prove otherwise?"

Soepenberg inserted pipe between lips and lightly puffed until dying embers came back to life, he contemplated Adam's words.

One of this blonde Boer's strengths was his devilish capacity to conceive one dastardly plan after another, seemingly in sequence without skipping a beat!

"Alright, what about blackmail?"

Normally Kok would've dismissed this succession of reprobate suggestions, especially from Soepenberg's rapscallion repertoire. However, the leader of the Griqua nation was desperate. At this point the coloured chief of Kokstad was willing to entertain any stratagem, no matter its palatability,

"Blackmail, in what form?"

Eyebrows rose amongst not only farmers but Adam Kok's ministers, surely decent and respectable men hadn't been reduced to so dishonourable a cloak and dagger enterprise?

"Doesn't he have a wife and kids coming with him?" inquired the white rat.

"A wife and I believe his niece will be staying with him at the lodge," replied Kok.

"Well it's simple, we kidnap the niece and hold her for ransom, a signed guarantee of our rights."

Adam Kok's nostrils flared, his upper lip curled towards them, you could imagine that during a countryside stroll Adam's sinus did chance upon the stench of a rotting hyena, "And I suppose you would be willing to carry out this nefarious venture on our behalf?"

Soepenberg straightened his back while plucking pipe from betwixt lips, "Aye, I would!"

Kok nodded his head in both agreement and disillusion, he whispered beneath his breath in a nonchalant tone, so only he and the good Lord might detect his words, "Of that I believe, of that I do believe."

Chapter Four: Sangoma

While Soepenberg deliberated on matters most foul, Jan and Arnou conducted business at the local store, Strachan&Co. An establishment owned by a pair of Scotsmen fundamental in supplanting the capital city of Kokstad from the foot of the Drakensberg Mountain range to its present day location.

A bell rang alerting the shop clerk to fresh customers, a Griqua and San. While peering upwards Donald managed to look down his nose, a feat only the white man had mastered to a degree it became part of his nature, "What do you want bastard?"

Now to be clear, "Bastard" was a derogatory term the white man used to describe Griquas. This moniker originated from the initial days of the Dutch East India Company on the Cape. Bred from lonely white sailors and locals in Cape Town Griquas were the product of white sailors/locals and Khoi-San females, enough came into being to form their own tribe named the "Bastards" by the white man.

Later on Cape Coloureds were stereotyped as being lazy and thieving, a justification used by white farmers in the theft of their traditional lands, an irony for sure.

Within a generation only Griquas and Khoi-San in the employment of white farmers inhabited the Cape area, pushed out by encroaching white farmers who later became the Boer. The "free Bastards" were forced further and further north and so Griquas, alongside white miscreants, hoping to improve their lot in life, made a trek coming to a halt in "Nomansland" or Griqualand East. An area made desolate by Shaka Zulu's Impi as a result of successive raids, its former inhabitants murdered or delivered to Ulundi in chains.

Jan sneered at the Scotsman yet spoke in a perfectly amiable tone, "Mr Soepenberg would like to purchase some supplies, if you don't mind Mr Strachan."

The short Scotsman wore a thick cotton shirt with sleeve holders sitting above the elbow. Despite the fact this fellow was quite wealthy and no doubt owned fitted shirts he wore a cheap one, employing sleeve holders so its cuffs hung about his wrists.

Over the shirt he wore a thick cotton apron with a small note pad and pencil inside, "I see, do you have a list?"

"I do," said Arnou as she stepped up to the counter, a scale rested on one side with a large metal till embossed with an intricate floral pattern on the other, Donald Strachan inhabited space in between.

Donald, a man with a horseshoe of hair on his head and clean shaven face peered over his spectacles at the tribal beauty, "Oh aye? Why don't you show it to me lass," he made a slimy grin.

Arnou smiled, "I cannot Mr Strachan, it is here," she tapped the temple of her skull with one of her long fingers, a beautiful talon ready to tear a man's heart from helpless frame.

Donald sneered, "A fuzzy wuzzy that can remember anything aside from when he gets paid and when his stomach needs filling? Why, this'll be one for the books!" Jan's right hand curled into a fist, his people had suffered the white man's vulgar insults, merciless acumen for business and theft of Griqua land long enough. To Jan these creatures from a distant domain shrouded in cold mist on the other end of the globe were white devils, especially the Scottish, for their ability to coin profit from a black man's hard labour was second to none.

This had something to do with the Scottish puritanical movement. In the past, education of children both male and female in the ability to read and write was enforced upon Scottish parents. No doubt accounting for the prolific nature of Scottish business ventures throughout the Empire.

Donald heard a creaking noise, similar to a ship's deck as its planks are stretched by Poseidon's seas. His vision switched to its origins ... he witnessed Jan's clenched fist, "Calm yourself laddie," Donald reached down and produced a shotgun, "We'll have no trouble in here." Jan unclenched fist. Noting a shift in Griqua demeanour Donald returned shotgun to its nest, beneath shop counter; always in easy reach should the Devil require employment.

"Now what does Mr Soepenberg want today?" the Scotsman replaced his weapon with a note pad and pencil, the tools of a Scotsman's trade.

"Ten pounds of Biltong please," replied Arnou "Biltong," Donald scratched his bald head before shouting into an open doorway behind him, "Hey blackie, is there any biltong back there?"

There was a hustle and bustle as someone searched a rear storeroom. Arnou detected pots and pans clang together until a young man found the object of his pursuance, "Yes sir, but we've only got kudu left."

Jan's face screwed up, "Kudu? Ain't you got beef?"

Donald's haggard highland hands stretched upon counter top, "What difference is it to you bastards? Your lot'll eat grass when you're hungry."

Jan was about to snap back but Arnou interjected, preventing a gentlemen's conversation from morphing into martial dispute, "Kudu will be very good, thank you Mr Strachan."

Kudu is an antelope which lives in this area of Southern Africa, venison in other words. The foodstuff known as biltong was a Voortrekkers creation, Voortrekkers being the Griqua led mob who trekked from the southern Cape, north then east to the eastern cape of South Africa, a trek of thousands of miles.

Requiring a food they might easily store yet remain fresh, they began to air cure meat, mainly beef, but game, venison and even fish were included.

And so Biltong became a staple food not just for coloured Griqua but the black San and white Boer. Why, in modern day South Africa, Biltong is sold across the country, known commonly as road snacks.

Biltong, a cured meat marinated in vinegar and flavoured with salt and spice has recently gained popularity across the globe, making inroads as far as the United States where beef jerky is by far the dominant cured meat snack.

Arnou and Jan spent half an hour at Strachan&Co's before requirements were fulfilled. The pair shifted sacked supplies to their wagon and Jan loaded them up.

The town hall meeting was on going and didn't seem close to conclusion, for men within did plot the kidnapping of the Governor's niece. They were to abduct then return her, unharmed, in exchange for a guarantee that Griqualand East remain untouched by imperial intervention.

Of course the fellows inside that town hall were unaware of the new High Commissioner for South Africa's disposition, his penchant for taking any situation of disadvantage and like a piece of clay in an artist's studio, moulding it into something not only pleasing to the eye but sufficient to one's soul, to such degree, this scheming sculpture doth demand royal honours in return.

The men of Kokstad remained equally ignorant of his new military officer, Major General Frederic Augustus Thesiger, a strict disciplinarian both on and off the battlefield, a man who if unleashed upon Henry's foe would savage the Empire's enemies as a lion might prey upon kudu. Gorging his face in open wounds while it lay helpless, fragile breaths escaping alongside the animal's spirit while the old bear Bartle caught up, joining his comrade in a succulent feast lay bare on African savannah.

Realising she might make use of her time in Kokstad Arnou turned to Jan and spoke in a timid tone, "May I be excused, I have an errand to run for Master Soepenberg." Jan fixed his gaze on the tribeswoman; her eyes glistening in daylight while suspicion filled his mind for Griquas did not trust San ... in fact Griquas didn't trust anyone, even other Griquas!
"An errand, I wasn't informed of this," replied Jan in a hard pitch.
"I need to visit the sangoma, for medicine, for Lady Hannah."
Jan let loose a sceptical sneer to which Arnou replied, "Very well, I am sure Master Soepenberg will understand."
"Fine," spat the Griqua, "but don't you be long or we'll both be fucked!"
Arnou nodded her head, "Of course."

Arnou stepped behind store fronts lining Kokstad's main fairway, making her way as fast as possible into slums.

Roads were filled with a dank dark fluid she was careful to avoid, since but leather sandals protected her feet. The streets were constructed of flattened earth yet successive rain storms had turned them into perilous paths rather than level pavements.

Huts were constructed of mud, compacted together with long grass, a very efficient living space for this region of Earth. Known to the British as an indus it has a single entrance with but a small opening in the roof so the occupant may light a fire within, pulling a mat or sheet off the chimney at the top to grant smoke an exit.

This section of slums was populated by San, each tribe allotting itself an area of hell. The stench was overpowering, for Arnou had lived as a house servant these past years and grown unaccustomed to her people's foul odour, the stench of poverty and deprivation.

Striding the settlement she garnered several odd looks, for though she was San there was something about the way she walked, head held high, proud gait attached to superior visage, neither Griqua nor white man had beaten the hubris out of this tall creature ... unlike every tribesman and woman populating this informal settlement.

Arnou asked for directions while moving through streets intertwining as branches on a thick hedgerow until resting at her destination.

Arnou, pulling aside a red cotton sheet poked her head within hut, "Sawubona?"

Inside was pitch dark, save embers of a fire at the hut's centre, long past their apogee, "Hello, is anyone here?"

From the darkness Arnou detected a noise and in the gloom, a pair of white globes hovered where a set of eyes might sit but these eyes were sheet white, those of a blind woman.

A crackling noise that mimicked wood as it snapped within flames exited an old crone who seemed to be multiples of Arnou's fickle years, "Ah, the eagle has come to roost."

Our eagle stepped within, not having communicated with this woman before today yet this young lady barely 20 years in age was puzzled as to how this creature identified her, for in the San language "Arnou" aside from a given female name is the word for eagle.

"Sit down little eagle, and tell me what you seek?"

The old woman was a sangoma, a spiritual healer who through contact with the ancestors might divine destiny and so heal ailments both physical and spiritual.

In the San community she served the same purpose as a local GP, healing hearts and mending minds whilst dispensing advice directly from the ancestors on how to proceed in life.

Arnou sat upon the floor, crackling embers of a fire divided the room, separating supplicant from sangoma. Smoke filled her nostrils, its aroma reminiscent of a cedar tree, burnt to sterilize the hut, its antiseptic smoke cleansed the sangoma's residence with virtue.

Being close to the fire Arnou now distinguished the sangoma from surrounding darkness, as light from glowing coals shimmered on pitch black skin her frame became embossed against residential gloom.

She was of advanced years, so many that a woman of Arnou's tender age was unable to decipher the extent of her maturity. The crone's hair was in a scrawny state, a dishevelled grouping of small dreadlocks with patches of skin between, a dark visage terrifying in aspect as light flickered against wrinkly old skin. While Arnou considered this creature's seniority a smirk appeared on melanin mirth, displaying a set of perfect white teeth.

Arnou's body lurched away from the juxtaposition before her, hiding behind cedar cinders.

The old witch laughed in delight at the young girl's shock, "Hah, hah hah, my form disturbs your sensibilities?"

Arnou took a deep breath, collecting herself she returned to her former position cross legged before the fire, "No, it does not."

The sangoma smiled at the girl, "Do not endeavour to shield my feelings from your judgement, I know you little eagle, I know you better than your own mind."

Arnou's crescent eyes formed slits as she scrutinized the old witch, her wrinkled body wrapped in a cotton sheet, naked arms touching knees. The eagle's tight vision noted golden bangles reflecting firebrands. The gold bangles were a curiosity, for Arnou wondered how they'd gone unnoticed on her initial entrance, secondly, she was curious as to how a poor old sangoma might come into possession of what looked to be at least 18 karat gold openly adorning her body on both arms.

Arnou surmised from the purity and number there was enough gold for the sangoma to move out of this slum and live comfortably.

"Hah, hah, hah," laughed the old crone in a mocking tone, for she took great pleasure at a young girl's curiosity and confusion, "You ARE an inquisitive one."

"My apologies," I was considering your jewellery.

"What of it?" smiled the sangoma, taking delight in youthful analysis.

"They are gold?"

A broad grin filled the sangoma's face, frightening our young San for her mien resembled a voodoo mask designed to turn the hearts of rebellious men into that of submissive children, "They are."

"Then I do not understand, why do you live here? In this slum?"

"Because here is where the ancestors instruct me to be, I am their instrument and must obey, just as you must obey, little eagle."

"I have but a single master ..."

Before Arnou might finish the undernourished crone interjected, "The white rat?"

"He is a lion, not a rat!" protested our young girl to which the sangoma chuckled, her grin reducing in size.

"No little eagle, but a lion is coming from a cold land beyond your imagination. He will arrive in Griqualand soon, he will lay the Griqua people low, crush the Xhosa and bring the children of Shaka to heel."

Arnou pulled a confused expression for such events were, as the sangoma had stated, beyond her imagination. Why to crush the Xhosa AND defeat the Zulu, two tribes who'd been in existence in one form or another since the beginning, since the ancestors first cast their gaze upon African soil, why, this prophecy could only be the insane ranting of a mad old woman.

Our eagle began to ponder the crone's legitimacy. Was she in truth a sangoma? Or just a charlatan using fear and superstition to make a living from local fools?

The sangoma, despite her lack of sight still had the vision to detect Arnou's emotion, for the spirit realm provides its own insight into the immediate environment. The witch's thin wrinkled body made convulsions of a humorous nature beneath cotton sheet, "Mami Wata does watch over her devotees."

Mami Wata is an African goddess specifically an African goddess of coin possessing the power to bestow good fortune and status through monetary wealth.

Arnou was sceptical of gods and goddesses even the one god of the white man for she had witnessed evil men plough wealth from the soil of Africa and its people, and she had yet to witness divine intervention upon their impious profiteering.

The old crone sensed hesitancy on the subject of gods and presented her forearms with fists to the ceiling, several gold bangles clanged together, "Then take them!"

The eagle drew its wings into its body, for she may have doubts over the truth in gods but there were many large burly men, San and Xhosa, living in this community and they were not averse to theft in the pursuit of improvement, yet these bangles remained on the blind woman's forearms. If those men refused to break in and steal her belongings it was for good reason, Mami Wata or no Mami Wata.

The tar witch returned her arms to lap, "Then speak little eagle, tell me of your desire to be with the white rat."

The eagle's eyes narrowed once again resembling those of a hawk swooping across African plains, searching for prey, "How do you know of my desire?"

"Your ancestors are watching little one, they warn you, the white rat's heart rests with the sickly swan."

Arnou sneered, "Why does Xu not heal her?"

"The white rat is a non-believer, he pays no reverence to his one god. Xu does not heal unbelievers, unless he has plans for them."

Xu being a god that lives in the sky, worshipped mainly by bushmen in southern Africa. His powers invoked in the healing of illness.

"Will she die?"

"That is in your hands little eagle."

"How so? I am not a god, I do not decide whether a man lives."

A smile appeared on the old crone's visage, "You are maid to the white rat's wife, are you not?"

"I am," replied Arnou.

"Then you have a choice," the witch put her fists forward and opened both palms, presenting two small leaves wrapped into separate balls. The sangoma pushed forward her right hand, "The blue leaf contains medicine blessed by Xu, it will heal your mistress," she pushed forward her second hand, "this red leaf contains poison blessed by Gaunab, it will end her life."

Gaunab being an evil god worshipped by the Xhosa, he is responsible for all misfortune including disease and death.

Arnou looked upon the red and blue balls, "Why?"

Our eagle was confused by what lay before her, not so much a misunderstanding of intentions but a conundrum of conscience for she was not an evil woman and up until this point had not brought mischief upon even the lowest of the creator's creatures.

Today she was offered a stark choice, heal the wife of the man she desired and be his house slave forever ... or ... murder the swan and become his lover ... and perhaps the lady of the house?

Temptation and temperance wrestled with one another in a terrible trial, a contest held inside every human being since Adam and Eve.

In her eyes it was possible to witness taught bodies ridged in darkness, for that is where the contemplation of evil takes place, whether it be an indus hut in the slums of Kokstad ... or ... it's town hall where men review the technicalities of hostage taking.

Within dark walls evil doth fester and multiply as a stinking black mould concealed from sun, orbiting a shaded rim encircling hell, a single breath enough to pollute a man's lungs sending him down into the fiery pit, the kingdom of Satan, the master of all dealings committed within shadows.

Our eagle's mind pulled back and forth between vice and virtue for there is no fence to sit on between heaven and hell.

She reached out and snatched both parcels, placing them inside a small purse. Searching inside Arnou produced a coin and replaced the parcels with cold cash.

The old hag cackled, "Hah, hah, hah, you are torn but passion will defeat principle young eagle."

"I have not made a decision," replied Arnou in a stubborn pitch.

The old crone scoffed at her rebuttal, "PAH! The ancestors scrutinize your future as the white man observes a theatre play. Heed my words, be careful little eagle for the ancestors love tragedy more so than comedy."

"I must leave, my master will be waiting," Arnou took the old witch's wrist and placed a second coin in her palm, "Speak to the ancestors, plead my case and I shall reward you."

The sangoma took the coin, shaking her head she replied, "Young eagle, the ancestors are not swayed by my voice ... for you, I can only warn, the path you seek to tread is littered with rocks and pools of water, tranquil sink holes do obscure torrid hell beneath."

Arnou nodded her head, "I understand, sawubona," with that our eagle departed this wretched roost, returning before the white rat finished his scheme to extend sovereignty.

The old sangoma placed both coins in a leather purse attached to a beaded belt around her waist. All the time she smirked before whispering, "So young, so beautiful."

Chapter Five: The Kidnapping

A steam train rolled into Cape Town Railway Station, built in the 1860's it was one of the Colony's initial terminals. Yet since this depot's date of construction, in 1863, the situation had drastically changed.

During the 1870's South Africa's first diamond rush commenced and in order to facilitate an ensuing corporate scramble the Colony's Prime Minister, Sir John Charles Molteno, pushed a policy through parliament, a policy of constructing railway lines across the colony, facilitating that very enterprise.

You see, before 1872 railways were built, owned and operated by private enterprise. Yet the push to Kimberly, a landlocked town occupying the centre of this colony's map, required responsible government to take charge in launching an effort to lay tracks to Kimberly and back to Cape Town.

Kimberly was a mining town with large deposits of diamonds being extracted from African bedrock in quantities unheard of in mankind's history, yet nothing but a wagon trail linked it to Cape Town, or any port city for that matter.

Considering that Kimberly was an equal distance from any costal port it was decided to drive a line straight to Cape Town and back.

During this period 1872 - 1905, the British built as if possessed by Hephaestus himself. Invigorated by a divine will they ploughed through desert, forest and savannah alike, there was nothing Mother Nature could do to block these white devils from their ultimate desire … diamonds.

In conjunction with supporting a flowering mining industry, the PM, John Molteno, focused a second drive to link African frontier for the purpose of military logistics; building main rail lines at Port Elizabeth and East London, two port cities integral when considering British encroachment on tribal and Boer lands east of the colony. It was at these towns a band of men boarded a train, first at Queenstown, an inland municipality on The Cape Eastern Line, starting or ending, depending on your point of embarkation, just south of Griqualand East.

From there they took a train south disembarking at Kingwilliams Town, from where they took horse and carriage west to Grahamstown on the Cape Midland Line, travelling south to Port Elizabeth.

Next they changed lines and moved north west, inland until reaching Graaf Reinet. Again the black and white band of scoundrels took a stagecoach west to Beaufort West, on the Cape Western Line, deep within the colony's interior on its western side.

Altogether a trip of three days by steam train, zig zagging across the Cape Colony; had they taken the same trip by stagecoach it might have been a month or more.

The final stretch lay on the Cape Western line, for the government had lain three main lines, Cape Eastern, Cape Midland and Cape Western.

It is alleged the Prime Minister drew up the Cape Western line himself with pencil and ruler on a map; Cape Town being cut off from its interior by a massive range of mountains known as the Hex River Mountains. By 1876 that obstacle had been surpassed by British ingenuity in the form of bridges and tunnels.

Cape Midland served Port Elizabeth, having acquired unfinished lines previously owned by the Uitenhage Railway Company the British lion quickly pushed north, linking with Graaf Reinet and therefore Kimberley and through a link between the Midland and Western Railways so Cape Town was now part of the British dream, made reality in only a few years.

The Cape Eastern served East London, another main port city, this railway was laid for purely strategic reason, its purpose to serve the frontier on the east coast.

The Eastern line had begun on August 20, 1873 when the Prime Minister turned the first spade, and within the same decade the line had reached Queenstown.

By 1885 the separate lines were linked up, bringing this epic endeavour to an end, the British had civilized another piece of Africa ... to a degree.

These railway lines led to considerable economic growth and development not witnessed before on the continent, bringing wealth and opportunity to those who lived within its interior and large sums of foreign investment to a land previously dismissed by outsiders.

Then in 1886 gold was discovered in the Transvaal, setting off the Wilwatersrand Gold Rush, but that is a story for another time.

Today a large hulk of steel ground to a halt in Cape Town, steam flushed the platform of a recently constructed station, yet its granite gave the impression of daily use. This depot facilitated movement of men and goods every hour of every day, with more than one platform, permitting a secondary train to stoke its firebox in preparation. A burly coloured man heaved on a large lever rising from the floor of a locomotive's driver room.

The handbrake eased off, steam began to escape hot boiler, shifting cylinders to strike as Vulcan's hammer, slowly at first yet gaining pace with gradual ease as the driver scrutinized instruments.

The coloured fellow pulled a handbrake back and released its catch holding the lever in place, wiped his hands then forehead with an oily rag as the engine left its station.

A group of ruffians looked across the platform after departing their train carriage. Jan's eyes engaged a Griqua train driver disengaging his brake.

No African would have been trusted with this fellow's responsibility yet Griquas held a unique social status here in Cape Town.

Unlike the modern day when a man of similar heritage would be considered black, in this age he was determined to be half white, an assessment deemed inappropriate by modern man yet on reflection it is by far the more accurate descriptor.

And so Griquas were treated in a fashion similar to a working class man in England. He was offered no privileges nor given benefit of the doubt. His motives always viewed with an eye of suspicion yet should he apply himself, work hard and so prove to be of value, he was as likely as any man of his social rank to succeed. This was something unique in British society, for up until now every society promoted a system of social order designed to keep elites on top while working class suffer underfoot, whether it be the caste systems of India and West Africa, or the class systems of Europe.

Yet the British were the first to make that valiant step into the light of God, break the shackles of slavery and offer every man, no matter his ethnic heritage a fair shot at becoming the success God intended him to be.

"What are you gawping at?" snapped Soepenberg.

Jan watched as the train pulled out, "I was looking at my brother."

"PAH! He ain't your brother! I bet he'd hand you in given half the chance."

Jan looked down at Soepenberg with a derisory glare, "We're not all charros."

The word "charro" being a slang term used to describe those of sub-continental descent, a title employed commonly in this region today, it is considered a racial slur.

Soepenberg laughed as their six man band of rogues gathered, five Griquas and Soepenberg.

Soepenberg, dressed in denim trousers and hat with a sheep skin jacket and cotton shirt yellow as chicken flesh, put his carrying bag down and lit his pipe with a match. He puffed until plumes of smoke rose, mimicking the train behind as it recuperated from a long journey across thousands of miles of rugged African country.

Removing pipe so he may taste African shag cured in his own barn, the white rat replied with gleeful expression, "Aye, you're right there, you can't trust them kaffirs either!"

As he spoke men and women exiting carriages after a long train journey glared at the course cur. Women dressed as typical Victorian ladies of this time, that is, a highly starched skirt, short of ruffles at the rear due to the fact this was not an event but a tiresome train journey. Waistlines just below the ribcage, tight bodice, hat, neckerchiefs to cover the breast area, although French women tended not to wear them but these women were British ladies; finally a light jacket of either matching or different shade to the skirt.

These ladies, whose ears had been assaulted by coarse Afrikaner tongue, gasped, placing one hand before an open mouth while the other tightened its loop around their husband's arm as thread gripping the eye of a needle.

Husbands raised eyebrows; older gentlemen displayed large mutton chop sideburns while dressed similarly to one another, that is, they resembled a character from 'A Christmas Carol'. The younger men were somewhere between Bob Cratchit and Fred, depending on their marital status. Elder gentlemen resembled a range between Ebeneezer Scrooge and the portly gentlemen who sought charitable contributions at the beginning. I suppose you could say that Soepenberg would have been a good match for Bill Sikes, nevertheless the rat observed how he and his band of cads did garner too much attention, he fixed his eyes on Jan, "Come on, get your bastaards moving, we can't hang around here." And so a heinous hexad lifted their luggage, a single bag to each man, endeavouring to exit platform and clandestinely creep into Cape Town.

On their way to an inn Jan looked around, he breathed in the stink of the city, its foul scent brought back favourable memories for this is where his tribe originated, the Griquas. Their initial moniker being "Cape Coloureds" for in the 17th century here in Cape Town they were seeded from a marriage between Dutch sailors, administrators and the local Khoi and San.

As they plodded the road, avoiding pools of ... well ... something; probably a run off from slurry generated via cleaning roads of animal excrement, for beasts were required to serve day to day city transport, moving heavy goods to and from warehouses, shops, the port and train station.

As they trudged through dirt, dung and deluge, Jan's eyes scanned the city, the home he knew as a boy.

Soepenberg was drawn to his coloured worker, on sensing a man taking pleasure from the world in which he lived, if only for a moment; the beastly Boer became irked.

Carrying his leather bag in one hand and removing chestnut pipe with the other, the Boer whispered so only Jan might hear, "Don't get all sentimental, we've got a job to do."

Jan was somewhat resentful toward his boss, stepping on a few moments of pleasure he'd permitted himself, for reminiscing on past times was one of few remaining pleasures in this coloured man's life.

Jan looked down upon the white rat, his visage pulled the smallest of sneers as a deep voice grumbled back like a bag of rocks tumbling down a hillside, "I haven't forgot."

Having found lodgings in a dinghy inn, our group of scoundrels prepared with a night's sleep and in the morning began scouting their target. Sarah Dixon, niece of Sir Henry Bartle Edward Frere, the newly appointed High Commissioner for the Cape Colony.

To track Sarah was rather a straightforward task; her movements never strayed from areas of what passed for high society on the southern cape of Africa.

She'd come to the Cape Colony in search of a suitor, as a snake in long grass hunting its prey. She sought, by means of stealth and venom, a man suitable for matrimony … that is … but a singular man sufficient for marriage, his name Major General Frederic Augustus Thesiger, heir to the Baroney of Chelmsford.

Added to that, Frederic's father lay on his death bed, not long for this world and so she sought to strike as quickly and cleanly as possible, for this man, on the verge of his fortieth year, had recently been widowed and was soon to become a Baron ... and she a Baroness.

Her uncle and aunt were practically in mourning for Frederic, for they were firm friends, their bond sealed many years before during the Indian Rebellion of 1857.

At that time Henry was in administrative terms a young man and though Governor of Bombay his grasp upon this prestigious posting was tenuous since natives had come to the consensus they'd rather it cut short.

He had to do something, so he turned to a recently appointed Lieutenant Colonel, his previous assignment the Crimean War.

Still a subordinate he served as adjunct to the deputy General yet distinguished himself many times in such manoeuvres as the breaking of the siege of Dehli.

You see, British forces were tied up in Crimea despite the war having come to a close, yet as soon as Frederic arrived with the 95th Derbyshire he moved quickly.

By the time he left India in 1874 and returned with his wife to England, he was an Adjunct-General with several accolades to his name.

After the recent death of Frederic's wife, a tragic incident due to a difficult child birth, he requested an open position of Major General serving in the Cape Colony, the commander of all Her Majesty's forces here on the Cape of Africa.

And so, based upon the intelligence of Frederic's impending arrival, slipped to Sarah by her aunt, Miss Dixon made haste.

Taking a ship from The West coast of India to the East coast of Africa, Sarah arrived in time to greet her prey as he disembarked a steamer from Bristol to Cape Town.

Sarah spent her days slithering back and forth between social clubs, events and wherever Frederic might roam. Not only did she stalk the General but made certain the Cape's other huntresses understood that this juicy piece of meat had been earmarked for her slaughter house. Yet unbeknownst to Sarah a band of bastards, led by a single white rat, shadowed the snake as she slithered through streets of Cape Town asserting dominance above lesser lion trappers populating a precarious urban jungle.

A pattern in her routine became coherent to Soepenberg's perception, for after one week of noting Sarah's activities on a piece of paper, gathering individual reports and Soepenberg's own witness on one sheet, the rat figured he might easily predict the path of this English viper over the course of the following week.

Added to that, her long golden locks and expensive clothing did permit straightforward discrimination when a jungle of beasts shifted within the same causeway.

A woman in her mid-twenties with these distinguishing markers was little challenge to hunt, and so they decided to pick her up on the way to the 'Victoria & Alfred Young Women's Institute'. A club for young women aged 16-30. Here they held social events, the older women taught younger married women relevant skills and trained unmarried women in tricks of the trade when snagging a catch, much as an old fisherman might teach his son how to bait a hook, where and how to cast and when to strike once an unwitting piscine did swallow his lure.

Ironically the club was situated at the Victoria & Alfred Waterfront, an area similar to Fisherman's Warf in San Francisco.

Sarah would frequent weekly meetings, however, rather than use it to train or be trained in skills concerning pursuance of prey, dissection and dragging him into church before consuming his corpse the next day, Sarah was here to assert dominance, reminding other women that the recently disembarked British lion was her suitor, directing Cape Town's fair ladies to forage in separate quarters of this colonial jungle.

Rather than taking her uncle's chaise and four Cape Town's sandy cobra would walk to club meetings. High Commissioner Henry Bartle did not approve of such insistence, each week he made a point of Sarah's folly in doing so, warning of miscreants likely to cross her path; for Henry was aware of the flotsam and jetsam staining the streets of the greatest city south of the African equator.

Yet today Henry remained oddly silent on her intrepid journey across Cape Town. Sarah thought nothing of it, for the cape cobra holds other creatures' concerns in slight regard.

Henry's wife, Catherine, was quite glad he'd finally let go, Sarah was in her mid-twenties and fully capable of securing herself for the short journey to the wharf.

Henry knew better, yet today this naturally foolish notion that a woman often holds to her heart for reasons that befuddle the male of the species would provide dividends.

Sarah strolled Cape Town's streets, head held high, asserting herself in the eyes of every other woman while avoiding foulness gathering in pools beneath.

She turned a corner, sedimentary stench quickly replaced with that of salt spray, fresh and succinct on the back of a South Atlantic breeze.

As Sarah walked a busy street, men moving goods while women shifted sundries, the cobra sensed something off and it wasn't the odour.

That feeling of dread which creeps upon an individual did envelop Sarah as a grey storm cloud might take a sailor by surprise. Relaxing in the sun, a warm drink in one hand, rocked to sleep by his boat, then Zeus cracks open sky, he looks up and catastrophe is at hand.

At least the sailor might take action yet in Sarah's case there was little to do, for a woman's intuition is strong yet without visual framework how might she act upon her feminine foreboding?

She carried on, catching a wide glance from left to right, unaware that a band of bastards scrutinized her every step, waiting, selecting the moment on which to pounce, as a pack of African wild dogs; animals that live in packs of 7-15, ugly in appearance and vile in nature, their dark smeared faces terrorizing other creatures during the night along with a unique call which rings as a bell to be detected over greater distance than any other animal cry. These creatures spread out behind the golden serpent before closing in, rubbing their paws, preparing the final moments upon which to snag their prey and whisk her away to Griqualand ... and then ... who knows what might become of this beautiful young serpent?

Burly wild dogs closed in as the street emptied of people, for many pedestrians in this quarter of Cape Town were Griquas themselves. Witnesses to the fact mischief did announce his presence and rather than be party to the Devil's work by virtue of mere observation they chose ignorance, for ignorance becomes desirable only once a man's eyes have been opened to life's evils.

This is why children are so inquisitive and why man and woman find them adorable. For a child is yet to witness the horrors which exist outside the protective bosom of its mother and so every new event is a delight, a chance for its parents to reminisce on a time before they knew of wickedness.

Each and every Cape Coloured disappeared into doorways and alleyways, draining the street as a tributary denying life from a great river after a band of men decide to build a dam upriver for their own villainous ambitions.

Sarah became alarmed as she watched men and women vanish from her gaze, each one reflecting her distressed demeanour.

The sandy cobra decided to retrace her steps, away from this beleaguered boulevard, and so in spinning around she was faced with a band of bastards.

"Grab her!" shouted Jan as five Griquas put their rough hands on a wobbly white woman dressed in perfectly presented blue day dress, white jacket, and feather fascinator.

The golden serpent struck out with her black purse, "UNHAND ME YOU FILTHY VAGRANTS!"

Soepenberg lifted his hand in a striking motion, his devilish intent being the employment of violence that it may produce submission ... a trade most mundane in his world ... then a whistle rang out.

African wild dogs were struck by the fear of God, heads spun peering back and forth as both ends of the street filled with local militia.

You see, a police force as one would recognise it today had yet to be formed, so several decentralised paramilitary groups patrolled Cape Town's streets rather than a centralized and properly sanctioned organisation.

The wild dogs of Africa halted. Sarah struggled yet failed to break free from their foul grasp, a grip trained in Soepenberg's fields via years hard of labour.

Then, from within a rabble of militia men, scarlet emerged as blood from the wound of a ravenous lion, its sight as terrifying as it was foreboding to this pitiful band.

Out of bloody scarlet a lion stepped forward, tall and immaculate, the epitome of a British officer in Africa, from his shining patent leather boots to brass shield on pith helmet, this white lion stood proud, glaring down a band of bastard wild dogs from the pits of Africa.

His beard, a pair of mutton chop sideburns intersecting upon his top lip, moved as the sound of fate made itself clear, "Gentlemen, unhand the lady."

At that redcoats either end of the street filed out, each end forming two thin red lines, the first set of men knelt fore, a second set stood aft, all four lines bringing Martini-Henry rifles to bear.

The British officer, cavalry sword sheathed on one side with Adams revolver plastered to the other side of his hip, was a daunting image, "Gentlemen, I will not ask again." On that every redcoat loaded a round into the chamber of his rifle, training his sights on one of the wild dogs.

African dogs released their prey, the sandy cobra hid her fangs as she ran into the white lion's arms. She shivered in terror at what momentarily had come to pass, tears pushed away from beautiful emerald eyes.

Some did speculate the cobra's tears to be manufactured, for Sarah was constructed of hardy grain. Truth be told, they were correct, for this was a most suitable circumstance, an attempted kidnapping only to be saved by her prospective suitor, why, a flurry of salt seemed a most excellent supplement to this scene.

Sarah wept into the breast of her soon to be beau, "OH, Frederic, thank goodness you saved me from those beasts!"

Frederic comforted his friend's trembling niece, "Have no fear Miss Dixon, you're in safe hands now," stated stoic lion.

She looked up into his cold grey eyes, grey for her, for they remained void of desire, life or spark. The death of Frederic's wife still lay upon his soul as the tombstone on her grave.

Frederic signalled his first officer, "Wood, take Miss Dixon."

Lieutenant-Colonel Evelyn Wood stepped forward exiting the firing line before accepting responsibility for the young Sarah. He ushered a sandy seductress back to safety, the cape cobra's eyes plastered upon her white lion at all the times.

Frederic's shadow fell upon a group of coloured miscreants, "Sergeant Bourne!" he roared, causing otherwise hardy men to steady themselves for his demeanour in tone was enough to force a large pack of wild dogs to turn tail and flee, yet these dogs had no option other than stand before an ominous onslaught. Sergeant Bourne and several of his most trusted men broke from the opposite end of the street to meet the central party, "Yes sir?"

"Take these dogs, we'll send them to live with the seals, or give them a jolly good hanging!" boomed Major General Thesiger.

When he said they'd live with the seals he was referring to Robben Island, robben being Dutch for seal. The island is within visual range of Cape Town and Table Top Mountain.

For more than two centuries it'd been a place of banishment, both a prison and leper colony. Robben Island also held many political prisoners, including Nelson Mandela who spent nearly three decades incarcerated there ... upon his arrival Mandela was informed, "This is the Island. This is where you will die."

After a few moments Colonel Wood interrupted, "Sir, these men must be given a fair trial."

Frederic pulled away, retracting his fierce temper from the fire box feeding a righteous locomotive. After releasing a deep breath and stabilizing his train of thought the General replied in a harsh yet decisive manner, "Why of course Wood, each and every man shall all receive a fair trial ... and then a jolly good hanging!"

From the corner of Frederic's eye the lion witnessed a rat slinking away, "You sir," the rat continued to move off "Sergeant, stop that man!"

Sarah broke through the lines, attempting to make it back to the lion.

Bourne grabbed the rat, spun it around, exposing its pitiful mien to virtuous British glare, "What is your business here?"

"Nothing," replied Soepenberg in a sharp pitch.

"Your hand was raised sir," replied Frederic.

"Aye, I saw these black bastaards going for that woman, they was going to rape her, so I tried to stop 'em."

Jan's eyes opened wide, "Liar! He was the ringleader, he recruited ..."

"Silence!" roared the lion.

"You ain't gonna believe that black bastaard over me are you?" stated the rat in an incredulous tone.

It was true, the rat hadn't laid a hand on Sarah although Frederic didn't believe a word coming from his mouth. Sarah intervened, "That man, he was in cahoots with them, I'm quite certain of it."

Frederic fixed his eyes on Sarah, "Please Sarah, this is no longer your concern."

Soepenberg snapped at her, "Aye, this is the business of men, not women."

"You'll hold your tongue, while in Her Majesty's custody," interjected Frederic.

"Custody? I ain't done nothing!"

Despite this character's villainous attitude there was nothing Frederic could detain him on and no prevailing cause granted warrant to stretch his neck, for military intelligence had pointed to a band of Griquas with no mention of a Boer, "Release him Sergeant but before you leave I'll have your name sir."

Soepenberg felt Sergeant Bourne's powerful grip dwindle, "Soepenberg, Bastijn Soepenberg."

Frederic's top lip curled as if his nose had detected a foul gust from Cape Town's sewers, "I shall remember that name Mr Soepenberg."

Chapter Six: The Poisoning

Morning broke on Soepenberg's farm exposing the fact relatively little work had been done these past days. For both master and task master were absent, hunting a Cape Town cobra in the name of Griqualand and her inhabitants.

Men shirked in decidedly shabby fashion, not the disciplined order one might witness should Soepenberg's eyes befall this lackadaisical excuse for labour on an East African morn.

Jan's mere presence always enough to stimulate slothenly slaves into rapid recollection of responsibility, the larger part of labour originating from KwaNatal ... Xhosa country. Formerly the Zulu's greatest, sorry ... I must correct myself ... for at this point in time the Xhosa were still King Cetshwayo's greatest rival.

Yet in a few short years the Xhosa Kingdom and its Chief, Kreli, would lay firmly in British hands, opening opportunity to a fully-fledged assault on KwaZulu ... a different story yet associated with this one insofar as the latter could not exist without the former.

But back to the present, in Griqualand East, on Soepenberg's farm. While Xhosa men rose in remiss, so San women did soar to their slice of servitude amidst the eye of Helios.

Amongst these avian creatures a falcon parted the flock. A beautiful and perfectly formed African eagle ascended to house duties.

It would be her burden to tend Mrs Soepenberg, check her temperature and change sheets while stoking a bedroom fire as the firebox of a locomotive, and her final duty … breakfast.

This morning, Arnou would choose her path, for it lay in Hannah's destiny. In her belt purse our San slave carried life in the form of a blue leaved ball, and death in a similar sphere dyed a hue of warning, red.

She remained in two minds, for our tall and tender beauty, that is, tender in years and appearance, understood her avenue of ultimate aspiration was jammed by a coach and horses, beleaguered by four sickly steeds.

A railway clogged by a convoy of corrupt carriages, to pass this junction her decision was clear, drop those red leaves into her tea. Murder the lady of the house and through a woman's guile, that feminine ingenuity residing within the heart of all females, she would swoop down upon a grief stricken rat, scooping him and his heart in her mighty talons, stealing the unsuspecting fool to her nest, where they might roost within a refuge of her love for eternity.

Or … she would post the cure and upon returning from Cape Town her master will have witnessed Hannah's recovery under the eagle's shelter. After which he'd realise who his heart was intended for and leave his white swan for a dark eagle.

Both scenarios, to those of us who have spent more time on God's Earth than a giraffe, do seem rather ludicrous. Yet to a young eagle with heart ruling head, these routes remained the only viable selections scoring her life's path; and upon consideration, a solitary option to these two scenarios emerged … to be wife to a man of the San tribe. When that thought did grace her mind the eagle pulled an awfully strained expression, as if battle were at hand. Our once soft and benevolent creature quickly transformed into hardy beast, betraying defiance and malevolence as conflict consumed her mind.

Yes, the thought of serving a San male caused Arnou's face to screw up as a child swallowing a spoonful of bitter cough medicine, her desire to spit it out overcome by the fearful gaze of a mother eagle.

No, Arnou could never submit to an inferior male, if she was to submit it must be to the white traders her tribe had mingled with since the 17th century.

When considering such synopses Arnou inevitably retreated into a Zulu proverb so she might reinforce, or justify, her stubborn stance. Like concrete, once poured, the quicker and harder it sets the better it serves its owner's purpose and so this old proverb hardened our eagle's resolve, "Umuntu ngumuntu ngabantu."

Which in English translates as, "A person is only a person because of other people."

Yet Arnou hadn't quite understood its meaning, for despite her fluency in Zulu she was not Zulu and so this nugget of African wisdom was reversed, from a reed to build a hut and shelter your family, into a stiff birch to lash the skin from one's own back.

For its implication is clear to one of the Zulu tribe ... an individual's strength comes from the group. This proverb emphasizes the value of teamwork and pulling together to meet a goal.

Unfortunately for Arnou our eagle took it to mean something quite different, rather than looking into the proverb and applying its wisdom to improve her decision making, she pulled and stretched it to cover a catastrophic course, as a sailor attempting to patch sail mid-storm with his own shirt, leaving his back exposed to Mother Nature's assault.

So Arnou's intent held fast, transforming this white rat from husband to widow to husband in an ouroboros of renewal.

Our San slave would remain above the clouds, hidden from danger as an eagle flies into winds during storm, fighting draft and blast to hover aloft, safe from sharp rocks and hard earth lurking beneath.

For the ground is where fate awaits and provided our eagle prevail overhead, lingering at the cyclone's edge she would endure.

The moment she and fate clash, she'd be destroyed, for Mother Nature would dash her against the sand stone of karma and granite of expectation, a concrete of creation hardened by sorrow, millions of years in the making.

"Lady Hannah is expecting her morning tea, hurry yourself Arnou," stated a fat middle aged black woman somewhat squat in appearance, wearing a black cotton dress, with white apron circumnavigating generous girth.

"Yes Aunty," replied Arnou, making her way to the kitchen where another San prepared breakfast for the lord and lady of the house.

Lord and lady being rather inflated titles for Soepenberg and his wife. Yet these were slaves, and so they addressed their owners with the greatest of respect.

Soepenberg remained in Cape Town on official business, that is all Arnou and fellow farm workers were aware of.

The rat and Jan's 'French leave' had left a vacuum. As their master's presence depleted so the Devil's did swell, for nature despises a vacuum.

This fact was no more prominent than upon Xhosa scowls and Malay masks, for a man's visage is a portal into his mind. San slaves and Griqua workers divined base brutality inside these creatures, encouraged by an absence of order alongside a growing sense of chaos, as its lord, Satan, did gather his powers amongst the foolhardy.

Nevertheless Arnou carried on with her duties for she was San, slave or not. Her people were of a higher order, they flew above the clouds where Lucifer's grasp failed to claw … that is, until today.

For while Xhosa and Malay did plot mutiny, so Arnou stirred tea within large ceramic pot. As dark char churned brown leaves caught in the flow of a swirling brew, so her thoughts were captured by the Devil, the sangoma's words swished through her thoughts as small leaves grown in a land on the subcontinent of Asia gracing African coast.

Active within our eagle's contemplation the sangoma's raspy voice echoed as a hyena in pitch black cave, "You are maid to the white rat's wife, are you not?"

"I am," replied Arnou.

"Then you have a choice, remain his maid, or become his wife."

Arnou reached inside her belt and scooped one of the balls with her smooth talon; she'd decided to leave it in the hands of the gods and so plucked at random before observing her choice via daylight cast from kitchen window.

Holding it in her right hand whilst stirring tea in her left Arnou was about to abandon her pestilent pellet to a swirling soak ... the eagle abruptly held her talon in place for her eyes caught a red tinge, hesitating for a moment our San considered possible outcomes.

Unfortunately, Arnou possessed an integral failing common to all human beings but most applicable to the young, that is a burning desire, or weakness, whichever angle of geometry pleases you most, to select the path of least resistance when considering one's ultimate goal. Her hand listed high above open teapot as a drunkard might sway back and forth attempting to reach his bed.

This dither carried on for what was no more than ten seconds yet in our eagle's mind the radius of time was pulled until it matched the diameter of the face of Chronos, causing his timepiece to inflate as an Africa twig snake.

Rather than hiss or rattle the twig snake will draw air into its nostrils causing its throat to expand. Across its serpentine spread conspicuous black markings are revealed upon the creatures head.

The creature alerts surrounding beasts of its deadly venom; a capable blood thinner that will destroy red blood cells within seconds of a bite.

Often used to ward off flocks of birds as well as land born animals, this is one of Africa's deadliest creatures and so for a moment, amplified in time, Arnou transformed from proud and honourable eagle into lowdown and treacherous twig snake.

Her conscience wrestled with itself, for our honourable eagle had not been fully expunged by satanic serpent.

In this moment of time two creatures engaged in mortal combat on African savannah, twig snake and eagle, tussling for supremacy while the sword of Damocles dangled above a bed bound Lady Hannah.

Footsteps could be heard, the heavy thump of Aunty's boots as she plodded towards the kitchen and so as the buffalo pressed near, eagle and snake split apart; for the buffalo was beyond both these creatures ability to mount a defence and survive.

And so they parted and in the kerfuffle, a ball of red medicine slipped the eagle's talon submerging beneath a dark sea of char.

There was a tiny plop and before Arnou decided on whether to retrieve the burgundy ball or not Aunty snatched the teapot lid, "What in the world are you doing girl?"

"I … I was making tea for Lady Hannah."

"It will get cold you foolish child!"

"Then please, allow me to make a fresh pot," requested Arnou.

"No, this will do. Besides, you know how the master is on waste," Aunty launched a skeptical eye in her direction, while the other sat on the teapot.

Aunty had a wonky eye and employed her so called "disability" to frightening ends. Young children hid behind mothers when the buffalo's gaze locked their meagre frame within her scope, as for adults, even Soepenberg found it somewhat disturbing which is why he made her head of the household. For Aunty's mere glance was enough to cause even a man such as Jan or Soepenberg to pause and consider his current activity.

Arnou nodded, "Yes Aunty."

The old lady removed the pot from our eagle's claws. Testing its heat with both hands she placed it on a tray, "Go, serve Lady Hannah's morning porridge and put a dash of turmeric in it."

"Yes Aunty," Arnou nodded as she cleaned out a ceramic bowl and headed to a large pot resting on hot stove.

An old iron pot was filled with porridge, kept warm the entire day and periodically topped up with water so as to prevent its drying out.

As Arnou ladled thick warm oats into a bowl Aunty delivered Lady Hannah's morning tea. Fear struck our San slave for death did make its way to the bedchamber as a train shunting into Cape Town Station. A thick cloud of steam rising while an evil engine chugged toward its final destination, pulling up at the next stop, before continuing its journey, carrying but a solitary passenger toward her final terminal, the underworld, that place from which even the bravest of heroes doth fail to re-emerge.

For only now did Arnou realise the folly in her actions, only when the deed was upon her did she lurch back from so devious a path, yet it was too late.

The Xhosa have a proverb, "Isala kutyelwa siva noolopu." Its meaning requires nothing but a direct translation into English, "A person who will not take advice gets knowledge when trouble overtakes him."

Wisdom of Xhosa elders began to overtake the foolishness of a young San woman as she watched Aunty leave the kitchen and head for the bedchamber with a carriage of contamination, moving at a steady pace toward its victim.

At that moment the sangoma's warning did ring inside the deepest grotto of Arnou's mind, "Heed my words, be careful little eagle, for the ancestors love tragedy more so than comedy."

The question was, were the ancestors laughing or weeping at this moment? For Arnou detected a sense of great urgency, she had to reach the station to which Aunty headed and prevent a catastrophe, before termination and destination collide, leading to where Helios doth refuse to cast his light, where Hannah will be transferred by boat to the land of the dead, to join her ancestors, with the one God.

The eagle quickly dashed turmeric on porridge and took flight down a hall, chasing Aunty's train as a hawk might move swiftly alongside a carriage, entertaining its occupants.

But Arnou was only human and when against the wisdom of ancients, this hawk, just as Prometheus, would be punished by the gods for taking what is their right, the destiny of mankind, into her own hands.

For it is a foolish arrogance of man and woman, especially in the coming centuries, who despite and because of technological advancement, see it fit they defy the gods. Believing themselves dominant as deities, using said knowledge to lift their brothers above those of others. Upon discovering the secrets of the stars and unlocking the helix of life, man saw himself as a god or at the very least, a god machine.

Today's scientist is no different from this pitiful San slave, the controller of an artificial product created in a jar, his feeble attempts at godhood sneered upon by ancient wisdom, since he becomes nothing more than the master of his own destruction, eventually he is forced before a jury of his ancestors, his sentence doled out by the one God.

All of this knowledge overtook Arnou in a moment; she did not understand what it was but sensed its presence via a woman's intuition and took flight in an effort to avert her own destruction before Lady Hannah might sip her morning tea.

But it was too late, for as she bolted in, attempting to defy the laws of physics and save her own wretched life, Arnou witnessed disaster; Lady Hannah was sat up sipping her morning char.

The secrets of the ancestors, for a moment, were etched upon the eagle's face as horror and tragedy clashed forming an inscription of evil and corruption, so much so she did frighten Lady Hannah.

Aunty witnessed the fright on her lady's face and turned toward the door, wonky eye connecting with a visage of true terror, "What are you doing child?"

Arnou was frozen, bowl of porridge in hand until it slipped from the eagle's talons, for Arnou grew limp as catastrophe's claws sunk in.

This African slave, like Prometheus, had angered Zeus. Despite her superior intelligence she'd committed a transgression, deciding to take the knowledge of the gods and use to further her own selfish ends. The great Titan, Prometheus, was tied to a rock, everyday his liver pecked away by an eagle, the creature of Zeus, the arbiter of omens both positive and negative.

Come night the eagle flew away, Prometheus' liver regenerated and the following day Zeus' creature returned.

Arnou wondered, was she to be punished not by Zeus but by Oya? The African goddess of fire and weather. For Oya not only controls the weather she also strives to seek out injustice and punish those who offer up deceit and dishonesty to the world ... and as for murder ... who knows what she has prepared?

For it is the residence of the gods to decide the fate of man, not a lowly woman's quarter.

"Clean up that mess and while you're at it, wipe that awful stare from your face!" snapped Aunty.

Arnou was transfixed, the power of the ancients holding her skull in place, forcing her eyelids open as a monkey might prize open a nut, coaxing soft innards into scorching sun.

Our San was forced to witness the evil she'd administered, her defiance of human law made visible via the light of ancient wisdom.

"Arnou! What are you doing!"

The eagle snapped upwards as it plummeted toward hard earth, narrowly avoiding a collision with Our Lord's callous crust.

Today she survived, this avian Judas employed superior mental acuity, a trait the San are most noted for, endeavouring to rescue her mortal soul from oncoming tragedy.

Perhaps Arnou could turn Lady Hannah's misfortune into her advantage, as two birds in combat, the powerful eagle took advantage of a beautiful swan's sickness and ripped it apart, not so she might consume this Dutch avian but conquer its nest, supplanting Hannah's roost for her own.

"Excuse me Aunty," our San slave exited before returning with a rag, dustpan and brush.

As she cleaned the mess Arnou's eagle eyes remained on Aunty, feeding the lady of the house a cup of contaminated char.

Slowly our San's expression transformed from one of horror to that of gratification. Unknown to Arnou the spirit of the Devil overtook her frame and made house, for our eagle had left the door to her heart unlocked ... agape to Satan's wickedness.

A warning to all men and women who tread God's earth; the Devil doth prowl this world, unseen as a lion, waiting for weakness and when he spies it he doth strike; an open door to a lowly slave's soul is red meat to the Prince of Lies and his unclean spirits, for she is constructed in the form of God and the Devil hates God.

And so the mighty Lord called out on his child's deaf ears, "Fallen, fallen is Babylon the great! She has become a dwelling place for demons, a haunt for every unclean spirit, a haunt for every unclean bird, a haunt for every unclean and detestable beast!"

Yet his mighty words went unnoticed for Arnou had been turned by the Devil. She glared, engrossed by the slow death of a sickly obstruction to her status as the lady of the house, her path to becoming something better than those around her, for Arnou was certain her destiny sat firmly opposed to that of kindred slaves ... unfortunately that place could just as easily be the fiery pits of Hell than the spiritual purity of Our Lord's Kingdom.

The Zulu have a wise saying, "Isala 'kutshelwa sabona ngomopo," its translation? "Who will not be told, will see by the blood flow."
But Arnou cared not. In her periphery vision she noticed a dark figure outside the house. Staring over Aunty's shoulder she witnessed the blind Sangoma grinning in the courtyard, standing beside bloodied tobacco rack with a patch of claret stained dust beneath her feet.
Rather than panic the eagle steeled herself while sneering at the old hag. Men walked through the courtyard of the kraal, Griquas taking time off work while slaves laboured in fields, an inactivity they'd not dare engage while the rat resided in his nest.

Our San's eyes tightened as crescent moons in the night sky, Arnou's deep brown eyes fascinated by what transpired.
Incredibly, grown men strolled straight past the old witch, chatting to one another while paying her no mind at all!
For a moment Arnou was shocked, the eagle lifted its wings in confusion for men who would beat any loitering slave paid no regard to the sangoma's permeable presence.
The wrinkled old shrew laughed at the eagle now bewildered by a rush of spiritual turbulence blasting her to and fro.

Arnou steadied herself, talons grasped firmly to the thick branch of a tall chestnut tree, for she refused to be taken by this foul bitch a second time, no, the eagle plunged deep within her own soul and brought to the surface a brand of fearlessness only women possess and spread it upon her body as moisturizing oil.

For men will harden their surface with gallantry and valour, and rightly so, for they are the superior of the species, blessed by God with natural physical power. Woman however, will pluck up a division of dauntlessness that seems foolish to a man. For she is unequipped to defend herself against the rigors of both man and Mother Nature, yet that feminine fortitude in itself is a shield, for like a peacock it has no great power over predators yet when they observe its feathers fan out and one thousand wide eyes peer back, many do take what they have and flee.

And so feminine daring can be just as effective as masculine grit.

"Arnou, what are you doing?" snapped Aunty.

"My apologies Aunty," stated our San slave, resuming her cleaning.

"Stop looking at those idle men and get back to your duties, you don't want to become a burden to Master Soepenberg, do you?"

Arnou crouched back down and resumed sweeping; she looked up momentarily, the eagle's vision fastened upon a semi-conscious Lady Hannah, sipping tea from Aunty's hand. Our San slave smirked and whispered so only the Devil might detect, "No, our master wouldn't want a burden in his life."

Chapter Seven: The Funeral

Soepenberg made haste, his steed pulled its carriage from Maclear to Kokstad as fast as its hooves might stamp earth. The African colt raised a dust cloud, these past months had parched native soil beckoning Boers into planting season, the devilish mare pushed hard while its master refused to spare the whip.

Soepenberg had barely escaped Cape Town in one piece, abandoning his faithful worker Jan and a band of brothers to swing on British rope, so on entering Kokstad relief remained his only companion.

On informing Adam Kok III of grim news Soepenberg noted an expression reminiscent to a bundle of rotten tobacco. The rat assumed he'd already been briefed, via telegraph or perhaps newspaper, since he was one of few Griquas with the ability to both read and write.

But nay the origins of this stack of spoilt weed, a cantankerous chestnut from the most blighted bush, were not of the aforementioned Cape Town checkmate, for Adam had already dealt with that disaster. No, this mention of miscarriage was closer to home.

For Hannah Soepenberg had recently been declared deceased; the cancer known as cholera had taken final victory in a conflict for his wife's mortal coil.

And so Soepenberg felt the onus of unfavourable news lift from his shoulders.

Taking Soepenberg inside his office, at the rear of the Town Hall, Adam insisted the tobacco farmer be seated.

The rat considered how his situation might further degrade, for he'd renounced his men to stand trial in Cape Town and when the harsh light of British justice fell upon its colonial subjects, man often met rope less than a month later.

The Boer had assumed that in the time it'd taken him to return, Jan and his crew had met a grisly end and this was Adam's method of breaking it to him.

Not that Soepenberg gave a rat's behind! He'd made it out with his own tail attached. As for those bastaards, there were plenty more hanging around Kokstad ... so to speak. Men who'd wasted wealth by selling allotments to fellows of cunning character.

Jan had been a friend or as friendly as was possible with Soepenberg, for this white rat held the entire world in contempt no matter its shade, white, black or coloured, regarding his fellow man no higher than a rat might view a hyena's corpse; ripping out soft juicy parts, dragging remnants back to his stinking lair, consuming carrion of all cultures for his own commonwealth of cowards, a community of but a rat and mute swan.

"About Cape Town ..." stated Soepenberg, yet before he continued Adam cut his flow as a beaver might dam a brook.

"Mr Soepenberg, please take a seat," the brown beaver gestured toward a seat upholstered in thick leather.

Soepenberg's eyes narrowed as a cheetah when wild dogs of Africa howl for blood. Unable to pinpoint position as bellicose noise rattles over night plains. The animal lays down protecting her cubs and waits for crazed creatures to pass, as a woman holding child behind skirt while drunken Griquas stagger the street, partying upon newfound fortune.

"Please sit," Adam remained sturdy while the Boer lowered himself into an armchair made from an equally rugged shrub, its tan similar to its owner. Sable and distinct, its leather a pleasant chestnut, age defined by many wrinkles life had deposited over the years, providing both Adam and his furniture a seniority amongst man and household movables, for does a leader not direct from the chair? If not so, for what other reason be he a "Chairman"? And so a leader's chair must be equally masculine in stature, its character and seniority a thing of power and presence; that is why men such as Adam Kok III owned these pieces, a necessary attachment augmenting his appointment.

Adam's armchair took the burden of its current occupant. Soepenberg's apprehension somehow lifted him, a weight loss of anticipation counterbalancing the toll of a journey to Cape Town and back while eluding permanent captivity, a lash to his back, or worse, the dead man's jig swinging on a length of hemp with coloured crooks.

"The British were waiting, they must have known, somehow," explained Soepenberg in an apprehensive tone for the rat contemplated whether he were sitting in this office due to Adam's ire. Soepenberg had no idea as to this creature's next words for he morphed between a brown beaver who'd built Kokstad and a warthog which when pushed is prepared to charge down another beast and consume its remnants. Adam's following statement hit Soepenberg as a train speeding to Port Elizabeth with goods bound for Plymouth.

"While you were in Cape Town, Hannah passed away," said Adam in a deep consoling pitch. He was used to informing citizens of death, for the Griqua nation's tale is a journey littered with corpses of men, women and children. He often noted that a Griqua farmer need not fear a failure in rain. He need but gather his tribe and recount their story, the great trek from Cape Town to Griqualand, and tears would feed his crop for another season.

"Passed away? Where?" rebutted the rat, his words attempted to parry a dreadful feeling which overtook his body, a demeanour of death encompassed the atmosphere. The chair Soepenberg sat upon took his full load as anticipation evapourated leaving but a void, and despite the Afrikaner's attempts it was permeated by distress, a terrible tide rushing in to douse an exposed beach in thick salt.

"In her bed, last month, while you were in Cape Town …
I'm sorry for your loss," replied the coloured statesman
enforcing truth upon another citizen of this new found
country, a nation formed through a trial of claret stained
catastrophe.

"But she was recovering when I left, she was getting
better … how?" the foul rat was adrift, for the only
woman he loved had slipped into a night no man, woman
or beast has ever returned from, save our Lord Jesus
Christ the Almighty who was now to judge her.

Adam was Christian first, and so occasions were rare that
he might permit curiosity or desperation to cause request
for ancestral counsel. The Griqua offered a blonde Boer
Christian comfort, "The dust returns to the earth, as it
was, and the spirit returns to God who gave it."

Soepenberg heard his words but they were hollow, for
this rat was a man of gold and accounts rather than God
or ancestors. The spiritual remained superfluous to the
substantial.

Unless something might be tallied alongside produce and
profit he had no interest. Unlike other Boers who at least
paid tithes and visited church on a Sunday, he did no such
thing.

Soepenberg would see Kokstad's church crumble as an
abandoned hut in winter rains before allocating a penny
of profit on its upkeep. The blonde haired, blue eyed rat's
pockets were where his principles resided in the form of
capital, which some might imply had been earnt via a
crooked path.

"Hannah's dead?" the words stumbled from his lips.

"I'm afraid so, Jan has been keeping her at rest until you return."

Jan de Villiers (rather than Jan Le Fleur, Soepenberg's former taskmaster) being a Griqua mortician who served both Kokstad and nearby farms.

"That bastaard's got my Hannah?" croaked Soepenberg in a lost tone.

You see the Griquas denotation of "Bastard" is incongruent with the westerner's dialect. For up until now those unfamiliar with this region of the world, ignorant to its ways, would conclude the term to be nothing more than a slur on a person's parentage, they would be incorrect.

For the true term "Bastaard" or as some would say "Baster" has a quite separate meaning in this part of the world.

The term "Bastaards" or "Basters" indicated a people with a higher level of civilization. More often than not they held a greater attachment to Christianity than the Khoi or San slaves who worshipped their ancestors.

The term "Black Bastard" in English is a wholly negative term due to direct translation. But these unfavourable undertones are solely a product of our own ignorance, for on the plains of Africa it conveys a different suggestion. This is why Griquas were denoted as bastards or in the Dutch "Bastaards" and "Basters". For they carried out skilled labour such as transport riders and craftsmen, setting them aside from other Africans; although the term was often used to describe Africans who could speak Dutch, ride and shoot.

As far as the hierarchy went, first you had Griquas designated as "Bastaards", then the San of whom Arnou was one.

Arnou remained close to her ancestors, yet she had the ability to speak Dutch and all manner of languages, along with the skill to quickly pick up a new language.

Then, as far as Soepenberg and the Boers were concerned, the Africans and Malays fell into place beneath.

Griquas were closer to their white forefathers than black mothers, taking the mantle of Christianity as well as other titles that went with being the first tribe of mixed race on the continent.

And so they employed a mortician rather than methods used by African tribes.

It had been noted many years before the British took control of the Cape Colony that African societies dealt with death very differently.

While the white man did attempt to cut ties between life and death, the black man did the opposite, enshrining his ancestors in everyday life so that essentially, the difference between life and death was present just as with the white man, yet the bond with his ancestors was not severed.

English scholars often noted the great positives of this practice, leading to stronger communities and a spiritual connection the white man has lost.

However, as with everything in Africa, there is a dark, bloody and violent side.

For instance, some African cultures become so entwined in the ritual of death they transform into something best described to the westerner as a death cult.
We have seen it play out in the modern day, take Kinshasa as an example, where for a time death was so banal the dead were no longer mourned, but life and death became one in the same.

A stunned Soepenberg was sucked into Adam's leather armchair, his body weak from crushing news filling his frame.
A sombre rat reconciled within while uttering not a sound, his wife, beautiful yet beleaguered, in his absence had been transformed into a plagued phantasm of her former self.
For the rat had no faith in the Almighty, he dismissed his ancestors and held little hope in humanity.
It was on the Great Trek, Soepenberg tagging on at the Orange Free State after selling his farm due to British pressure. Hitching his cart to a Griqua horse and journeying into the interior of modern day South Africa, that this where this man not only lost faith in God, but learned to rely upon himself.
For as Voortrekkers pushed within, corpses of those who believed in Christ, ancestors or both did fall by a dusty path named destiny, their bones converted into gruesome milestones marking a terrible trail into African hell.

Black, white, rich and poor, man, woman, child and cattle, their saviour never came. Yet a man devoid of Christ pushed on, maintaining his lack of belief as a hound might disguise hatred for its master, only to one day let it boil to the surface and rip his master's breast, the hound's owner never understanding he'd nourished calamity rather than faithful canine.

So the Boer couched contempt deep within, preventing it from rising to the surface, holding hatred within, for now. "Funeral arrangements have been made, I hope you don't take me as presumptuous," noted the coloured statesman.

Soepenberg pulled out of his malaise and locked eyes upon the Bastaard chieftain; he failed to push a sound from his breast, for this news did weigh upon his chest as a sleeping rhino.

Hannah, the only commodity Soepenberg possessed that couldn't be bought or traded for gold, the only item of value curbing his temperament, as a wild dog leashed to a stake in the ground. Cholera had rotted that stake, turning it to dust, indistinguishable in a trash laden yard. The rabid beast escaped its chains and was set to pounce upon the first trespasser.

"I was unsure if you'd be returning from Cape Town. We received reports of men captured, but no description, did they take Jan?"

Rising from the doldrums of depression for a moment, as a diving bell does break calm cold waters of fate, light returned to blue eyes and life his face, "They got him," replied the white rat with a subdued squeak.

"Got him?" inquired Adam.

"Aye, I reckon he's had a hemp collar fitted by now."

"I see, and your men?"

"Dead, all of them."

Adam failed to raise an eyebrow for death was a daily associate, especially during the Great Trek.

Perhaps Khoi-San ancestry had blessed this warthog with the sensibility to negotiate Hades and his dark kingdom? For he lived with mortality rather than grieve, Adam's African heritage the superior when required.

Much like a battle, when necessity demanded, Adam's European heritage did load rifle, take aim and fire into a frightening assault off horrors thrown his way, whether that assault be white cavalry or black spear and shield.

Conversely, when his African heritage outweighed European in usefulness, spears and shields were broken out, the drums of war beat and raised his soul, steeling temperament and casting courage. Tribal instinct took authority, warriors charged, overwhelming a situation of extermination via superior numbers and superhuman courage.

"That is most unfortunate, Jan was a decent man by all accounts," commiserated Adam.

"Aye, but Hannah, how did it happen?"

"Last Tuesday morning, Hannah passed away shortly after breakfast, you'll have to ask Doctor Albronda for details," replied the coloured chieftain clasping hands atop the table.

Adam was familiar with death yet its presence often pressed upon him, it was only after many years of lifting progressively heavier weight that he carried Soepenberg's burden with ease.

"Aye, I'll speak with the doc," replied Soepenberg as a man lost at sea, buffeted from one wave to another as the Devil mocked another fallen soul.

"Mr de Villiers is awaiting your signature. I'm sorry to press you so soon but her body was to be released and put to earth today."

"What?" asked the Dutchman in a growing tone, increasing as the Devil entered his frame, lending the power of a demon and fortitude of a fiend.

"It was ascertained you would not return in time to bury your wife, her corpse cannot be permitted to remain within the mortuary any longer."

Adam was referring to the fact that in this day they had no means of refrigeration. This was a frontier town in a frontier country, a corpse must be buried before it decays, spreading its malady to the population.

"Corpse? That's my wife, not some dirty black bastaard you can chuck into a pit fifty at a time!" snapped the rat as Satan delighted, pulling the heart strings of a sensitive servant.

"I'm sorry for your loss Mr Soepenberg but in my business an infected corpse must be disposed of quickly, be it black, white, rich, poor, king or slave. Our Lord and Saviour Jesus Christ does not discriminate," the coloured chieftain pulled a visage as serious as his tone, forcing Soepenberg's Devil into retreat … for now.

The mere mention of Our Lord Almighty doth persuade the prince of lies to pause in his miserable machinations. Even in the bowels of Hell, a man might speak his name and demons will scream in pain, the undermost utterance of our father sending shockwaves across the fiery pit.

Similar to a volcano resting on the seabed, imperceptible to man while hidden beneath dark ocean gloom, it detonates with all of Mother Nature's fury during her greatest of tantrums.

A blast wave becomes visible from a great distance, water transforming to steam before revealing a wave of righteousness, fast approaching the sinner, bound to wash away filth and degradation.

And so, for the moment, the Devil's appetite was abated by fear of God. Yet in the perception of Soepenberg he'd merely changed demeanour, regaining his sense of balance.

"Aye, aye," noted the white rat in a somewhat stoic manner.

The Boer produced his pipe, stuffed it with African shag and fired its brown leaf in a robotic fashion.

Adam's eyelids tightened to form arrow slits in their brown stone wall. He was a firm man of God and the Bible does instruct one to treat one's body as a temple. Such activities as the consumption of alcohol and tobacco are not in the remit of scripture.

Why the churchwarden style of tobacco pipe is said to have originated in the new world, when man first took the brown plant into daily life.

The function of its long stem being not only to cool tobacco but when in church the priest did often request worshippers not smoke, to be met by the reply "We cannot."

And the churchwarden was born, a pipe that might rest outside the church via a window whilst permitting its owner to worship within ... but on to matters in Kokstad.

A man was in mourning, a wife was to be buried and somewhere a slave's Machiavellian stratagem was being prepared as a potjiekos, a traditional South African stew. Rather than a refined meal presented at an upper-class dining table it was a mishmash of meat, beef, lamb, chicken, venison and pork, with vegetables cast into the same three legged pot, known as a potjie. Its contents tossed in as a fisherman might bait water.

This meal, common amongst slaves and lower sorts often comprised of leftovers from the master's table.

So her scheme, with meat from the sangoma and hot coals of the eagle's heart did take form in a somewhat clumsy manner.

As the master buried his lady wife, Arnou plotted her next step, to take her seat at the dinner table. Yet, as is common with man and woman, the power to destroy always comes first since it is the most accessible and quickest to administer.

For it is simpler to destroy than build and as man doth progress in the future, inevitably his adeptness at destruction is honed until he wields the sharpest blade on planet Earth.

One day, he will possess the power of the great titan Pallas, father of Zeus and Nike. Man will manipulate the capability of the Gods of war ... yet fail to acquire their wisdom.

And so our San slave had fallen into the same trap, holding the sword of Damocles above Lady Hannah she failed to access the foresight necessary to wield such responsibility ... her ancestors aware of this folly did their best to dissuade our young eagle.

Another ethereal being was aware, for Satan moved from his Boer host, shooed away by mention of Our Lord until he discovered safe harbour in the dark heart of a misguided eagle.

Flying high above the savannah of normal life, Arnou's unique capacity for cunning pushed her aloft on thermals of sage prophecy; for the eagle believes itself above all other creatures, the white rat, the golden snake, grey horse and dark coloured east African wild dog.

All of God's creations seem insignificant to her, wings spread, coursing cool atmosphere, superior to all ... yet the eagle only looks down, where its prey dwell.

For above the eagle do rest her ancestors, watching down and above them are the gods and still higher Our Lord and Saviour Jesus Christ the arbiter of fate, the final adjudicator in the trial that is life, her ancestors the jury, Arnou the accused, but that all appeared superfluous while the eagle monitored her prey, scurrying back and forth, seemingly at her mercy.

The sickly swan barely able to move, she swooped down to take its life while ancestors shook their heads, as if she were killing her tribal totem.

That is, many tribes in Africa have an animal as their totem, a spiritual guide. To kill your tribal totem is an error of life changing proportion.

African tribes possess different totems and so their views on animals populating the Dark Continent change tribe to tribe.

For instance, in Europe the lion is considered king of the beasts but in Zululand it is not so. This powerful feline, rather than a king is a judge who weeds out the weak by consuming them and separates the dangerous by killing them.

The Zulu believe the lion is both meat and grass eating and thus unites the two worlds of carnivore and herbivore, judging all on the plains of Africa.

As for the eagle the Zulu consider it to be one of the oldest, wisest and strongest creatures in existence. The Bateleur eagle, or as they say it, "Ingonghulu" is a sacred animal. When the Zulu creator planted the tree of life the first creature to emerge from it was Ingonghulu, announcing his birth with a terrifying squawk. And so the Bateleur and Black Chested eagle have been recognised as sacred animals and a creation of God; and so our San slave, a sacred creature of God had committed a foul deed by slaughtering a regal swan, angering that same Zulu god, who in rebuke did implore the Almighty to secure sacred arbitrage.

Chapter Eight: Leopard Lotus

The heavens dispersed life giving rain upon dead ground, beating dust into wet mud. Yet Reverend Dower remained on point, beseeching Our Lord prior to bequeathing Hannah's body within the earth it came from.

Hannah's choleric corpse was wrapped tight in linen and doused in coal tar before placed inside its coffin.

Soepenberg had been denied the opportunity of viewing his love before her last rights. Not only that but he was refused the luxury of a grave, for she was buried in a pit, a cholera pit.

Eight feet deep and sprinkled with quicklime, her coffin was placed alongside others in a tainted tomb.

Soepenberg protested, he'd tried persuading Adam to release her corpse so he might bury his wife on his farm, the statesman refused. For this plague was a virulent killer and required utmost vigilance.

To release but a single victim's corpse for burial would be foolhardy, should she be laid to rest on a farm there might be uproar, certainly Soepenberg would go out of business and fail to sell his property, for no man in his right mind would purchase a farm or its produce while cholera victims lay entombed within its soil.

Of course, at this point in time people were unaware that transmission was solely via contaminated food or water and these cholera pits served no practical purpose other than to becalm local logic.

Nevertheless, that function was of paramount importance if this settlement and Adam Kok's leadership were to be successful.

The Griqua people had suffered enough, drifting to and fro across Africa, now was their time to put down roots and stand against the wind as an acacia tortillis, otherwise known as the umbrella thorn or umbrella tree, its distinct form reminiscent of an umbrella high above savannah.

Its bark rough with a grey to black colour, its thorns similar to a pike staff, one straight thorn growing in combination with one hooked.

Its flowers form in clusters here and there on old wood in creamy coloured balls. Its pods a distinct golden brown, its leaves are very small giving it a soft almost feathery appearance.

In many ways this acacia represents the Griqua better than anything else in Africa; they are present on every part of this fern.

During winter it blooms, sporadically, depending on seasonal rains. Its flowers, like the white man, attract the black eagle yet its white thorns deter many other creatures.

When the tree is young browsing birds have a light task collecting its produce, for thorns are soft and pliable while in development.

Aged thorns guard more fruit due to the fact they're hardened and tough and only the toughest avian dare bridge its barbs in order to reach the most succulent fruit on a thorny umbrella sitting in Nomansland, renamed Griqualand East.

For these were a people who lived where white and black feared to venture, cultural castaways squashed between the spirits of African ancestry and sanctity of the white man's saviour.

Soepenberg had become one of them, or as much as a white man could. Through the loss of his wife a bond had been severed between him and the world of the white man, that day he transformed from Boer to Afrikaner; no longer bestriding this planet with both feet in the realm of the Boer but one firmly resting within the African's domain.

He did business with white men, employed Africans and Asians on his farm and was subservient to this lands coloured ruler; it's no wonder South Africa today is one of the most confusing lands in the world, to both black, white and coloureds.

So it's easy to understand why at this time war was rampant, violence common place, races vying for superiority over resources, over tribes, and when the rains failed ... blood did bathe the plains until sufficiently soaked that grass began to grow and cattle fed once more.

Soepenberg watched on during this rainy day, moisture raised an odour from sodden earth, the stench of death, as his wife was lowered into her pit along with several other cholera victims, for she was not alone.

While their ceremony took place, women crying, men sombre, umbrellas providing shelter, a black eagle observed from far away.

Peeping from within an alleyway in the San quarter of Kokstad she scrutinized her prize. Arnou felt rain beat upon her skull yet our San slave paid no mind, for her prey was at hand.

Dressed in tribal leather skirt and crop top, rain removed dust, sky drenching her in purity as she smiled. Lips stretched until our young hellion felt the Devil rise within her, for mayhem was at hand.

While focusing on a white rat which Arnou planned to hold fast in her talons ... a dried tone took our slave by surprise, "Calm yourself young one."

Arnou spun around and in the dark two floating eyeballs, sheet white, peered through darkness.

The old hag cackled with delight as she sensed an expression of shock fill the visage of a young woman, a visage that over these last days had lost its innocence by degrees.

For the Devil had found lodgings, corruption chasing out chastity, sincerity bogged down in a swamp of sin to such a degree Arnou felt her heart heave while her body soared from its morning roost.

With each passing day the murder of Lady Hannah become a greater burden yet Arnou had cast her die and but a single option remained in our young slave's mind, double down, press on, push for the summit of immorality with but a blind sangoma and her own lust as guides.

Our San steadied herself by gripping the rocks of vanity jutting from an edifice of a mountain of misdeeds while winds of bewilderment passed her by. Asserting herself Arnou replied in a defiant tone, "What is your business here?"

A set of yellow teeth made their presence known, somehow on this dull grey day in Kokstad all light concentrated upon this witch before the crone cast it upon Arnou, exposing her crime.

Much like a spotted gennet, a common creature on the Eastern Cape and around Cape Town; pale grey in colour, they have small spots and a stripe running down their spine to their tail, the long tail covered by rings of black and grey. Often mistaken for felines they are in fact viverrids, a more primitive version of a feline.

A rough prickly tongue, four to five toes on each paw with half-retractile claws. It comes out to hunt at dawn and dusk, a skilled climber it stalks the lowest snake to the highest bird and all those between.

Its name is derived from the Latin for ferret, "Viverra", and though some may have similar features to a ferret, the two are completely different creatures.

Well, the old sangoma did resemble a gennet, her bright eyes gathering all available light before casting it upon her prey, primitive jaws and a prickly pink tongue. The primeval hunting the reprehensible, "It is the business of the ancestors, I am their vessel, they brought me here to witness your foolhardiness."

Arnou lobbed a snobbish sneer as cannon might fire shells at a line of advancing Zulu warriors, yet much like the Zulu, death was not a threat this wrinkled witch feared, let alone an angry child, "Ungalibali intaka yobusi," stated the wise woman.

"Ungalibali intaka yobusi," is an old Xhosa proverb, its translation? "Don't forget the honey bird," its meaning? It means to say that you should not forget to give the honey bird some of the honey that it helped you find.

Arnou lost her miserable demeanour yet her voice maintained its vice, "You have already been paid, generously, do you want more? Perhaps you are an extortionist rather than a soothsayer?"

The old woman's demeanour morphed from amusement to anger, our young lady felt fear rise up past her heart to strike her head as words lashed from bristly tongue, "Ukasela eziko."

Its direct translation, "You are creeping on your knees toward a fireplace."

Its meaning? It is said in reference to a baby shuffling on all fours in a hut toward its centre, where the fireplace does sit. The proverb signifies that you're heading toward disaster if you continue along the same path.

"Hey!" roared a voice from behind, Arnou spun around and there stood Soepenberg striking something of a mood.

Arnou was caught in crosswinds, our slave's limbs barely held onto her self-constructed fell of fault.

"What're you doing?" snapped the white rat as his San slave looked around in a discombobulated fashion, caught between sangoma and master.

"I erm, I was …"

Soepenberg looked behind Arnou for his slave was attempting to hide something, "What's going on?"

"Nothing Master."

Soepenberg pushed Arnou aside in a brash manner, "Don't sell me a dog," ("Don't lie to me") the alleyway betrayed nothing out of the ordinary, yet he was certain she'd been chatting just moments ago.

Arnou turned to witness clear space but considering the distance covered by this alleyway, with nowhere to turn off, left or right, it was not possible for even a trained impi to sprint to its end and make an escape in so short a time.

Our San slave narrowed her eyes, peering into shadows where this dark gennet might align itself, employing shade to obscure shape, yet the old woman could not hide from both Arnou's eagle eyes and the white rat's night vision.

Soepenberg turned a suspicious eye upon his slave, "Well?"

"I was speaking to the ancestors, imploring they ease Lady Hannah's passing," blurted our scheming slave.

Soepenberg double checked the alley before rebuking his house slave, "Get in the wagon, we're going home."

Both man and woman observed one another in an awkward moment of silence, somehow through the dank drizzle of death the pair sensed a connection, a spiritual force pulling two opposites together.

Unlike others, pro and epilogue, these were not soul mates, for their attracting force was lust. A barbarous desire of master and slave to mingle with one another, a strange concoction as old as mankind itself, a mixture of fascination and yearning, like iron and carbon, two totally different substances, when fused together inside the Devil's forge of passion they merge to make an alloy harder than common metals provided by Mother Nature. Just as fallen angels interbred with the purity of mankind to create the Nephilim, a tall, strong being, a hybrid of the two.

Both these children of God had fallen and their lust was set in stone, the ancestors reciting this judgement to the sangoma who passed their divine decree informing Arnou … but was this sangoma truly in contact with the ancestors … or something else?

Nevertheless, our eagle was fallen, not in flight but in spirit and would suffer the consequences. Soon the melding of man and woman would cause a cataclysm, starting a chain reaction that would lead to the capture of Chiefs, the descent of Kings and the defeat of a great tribe.

Soepenberg's crystal blue eyes wrestled with his brow, sweating under pressure as the bow of a blonde canoe bearing down a lake's clear waters.

His hands became tense, gripping onto something yet its form eluded Arnou; what was this sensibility he did grapple with, hatred or hunger? Perhaps both? These emotions being brothers in barbarity, the white man as barbarous as black despite his protestations and declarations of gentility.

His forearm flexed beneath a white shirt as droplets of water splashed upon linen, our San slave felt a perverse attraction, something moved fast between her heart and vagina, even in this cold rain the core of her body heated as the Devil ordered demons employ greater force upon the bellows of lechery, increasing in rapidity moment to moment while the Prince of Lies cast his head back in laughter striking a hammer named desire upon an anvil of acrimony, base beats sent sparks of evil eroticism spinning between master and slave, an immoral aphrodisiac.

The two were secured in one another's orbit, master and slave, Earth and Moon, man and woman, white and black. Unknown to Soepenberg the Devil in Arnou had taken her to a local herbalist where she'd purchased a plant famed for its qualities in attracting a mate.

The leopard orchid, one of South Africa's most beautiful flowers and one of the largest orchids in the world.

Its five petals, unfurled in a star, are yellow with brown spots giving the Ansellia africana its name.

This flower does grow high up in trees, taking its place within the black eagle's roost. Its flower is famed across Africa for its beauty yet its aphrodisiac is contained within not its exotic blossom but its cane and roots.

The catch is that the leopard orchid only becomes suitable for muthi (African medicine) after ten years maturation. There are many large clusters of these orchids to be found up high in the tallest umbrella ferns, as old as fifty to one hundred years.

Yet this love potion comes with a stark warning, often the herbalist selling this muthi will caution its purchaser, asking if they're certain the person they wish to attract is the right one for them.

Arnou had purchased a potion from the local muthi peddler at some cost; she'd only just smeared it on her chest before the wagon ride home.

The eagle would sit next to her prey as usual, its scent enchanting the white rat. Until now she'd kept well away from other individuals at the funeral, standing in an alleyway, and as planned Soepenberg approached and ingested a whiff ... it seemed to elicit the desired effect.

"Hey boss, the men are ready," stated a Xhosa who'd taken Jan's station until Soepenberg might employ some Griqua workmen.

The slave's Afrikaans wasn't good but it was sufficient to take orders, though Soepenberg found himself leaning on Arnou throughout this difficult period.

Soepenberg's momentary vacant expression vanished. He turned to the Xhosa slave, "Is the wagon loaded?"

"Aye boss."

"Then get in the back with the other kaffirs!"

"Aye boss."

Kaffir being Muslim for not only non-believer but someone of an inferior racial or cultural background, this term was used widely in Southern Africa as a slur. Outsiders often forget that Middle Easterners have a sizeable presence in this region of the world similar to that of the white man.

Soepenberg pushed past his Xhosa slave, Arnou followed Soepenberg, the dark skinned fellow took a deep breath and in that moment the scent of seduction took him, rain dripped down his face while his lips surged, meeting his African nose, tribal eyes stalked as a hungry hyena would trail a wounded fawn.

Arnou stopped, turned to him and snapped, "What are you looking at?"

"Amathe nolwimi," replied a leering youth. His eyes ground inside his skull while arms reached out and grabbed Arnou by her forearms.

Now the idiom or phrase "amathe nolwimi," when directly translated into English means "Saliva and tongue."

It is an expression used by the Xhosa to mean two people who are inseparable, but in this case, after one has taken into account the Xhosa youth's seedy visage and forceful actions, the phrase does contain rather obtuse sexual connotations.

Before it went any further, the young Xhosa captured in the grasp of satanic seduction was awoken from his lust by a horse whip across his back, "Aye! Get into that wagon you useless kaffir!"

The blow reminded him of his station and the fact he was attending the funeral of his master's wife.

Arnou shook free as the fellow's brain was pulled between coherence and cock, she delivered a mighty slap on his jaw flipping the Xhosa youth's concentration … igniting rage in his eyes. A glow of lust transformed into fire and fury; he made a fist to beat her down until an equally lusty lash tore his shirt, "Touch her and I'll have yours and your mother's skin!" roared his owner after a flesh splitting crack echoed up and down a damp roadway where mourners emptied from the churchyard having walked some distance from cholera pits administered by Reverend Dower.

"Mr Soepenberg!" stated Reverend Dower, raising his voice. Neither rat nor eagle believed this bearded Scot was capable of such a stiff temperament. For this tall dark haired man often demonstrated the sublime, never straying from the good book, he refused to exhibit pride in anything but the Almighty.

His hair was as dark as the niger seed, a small black seed the Reverend fed to his birds, originating from the Guizotia flower, particularly loved by gold finches.

His wife close behind, dressed in mourning attire, often complained that the colour black took up half of her small wardrobe due to the many deaths she was obliged to attend.

Jesse Edward Dower, the Reverend's wife, a stern woman, hardened by life as the wife of a missionary, often dreamt of the high life in Cape Town. Far away in the civilized parts of Africa where the British had planted their flag, emancipated slaves, built railways, roads and other great structures that would stand the test of time. Women did dress in wonderful colours, attend fabulous balls and dance with dashing young men who fought barbarians, risking life and limb for the glory of the Empire and the love of a woman.

She'd expressed this opinion in her husband's presence, only to receive a reply in the form of the Reverend's signature fire and brimstone glare. Jesse felt the Lord reverberating throughout her body and quickly apologised for such a fanciful notion.

Her husband, the good Christian he is, forgave her with equal rapidity.

The Reverend's family originated from Aberdeenshire, Scotland. He himself had followed his father into the family business, construction. From there William went to Edinburgh University on a bursary and was ordained as a Congregational Minister. William was appointed by the London Missionary Society as a Wesleyan Missionary in South Africa and so he and his new wife Jesse, set sail in 1865.

In March 1870 William and Jesse went forth by ox wagon journey to East Griqualand and the town of Kokstad, where he was asked to take on the role of pastor.

William drew plans for his first family home in Kokstad and did much of the building himself, completing it in 1871. The windows and doors were made by his father and imported from Scotland. The building still stands today and is now a craft outlet.

The church building was also built by the Reverend Dower, in the Gothic revival style of the time; it has beautiful examples of woodwork bearing testimony to his skill as a carpenter.

Arnou always thought of him as a melanistic panther, that is a black leopard. A quiet and calm creature yet if challenge he'd tear his opponent apart, not by violence but faith in the Lord, invoking Lord Jesus Christ to his side, causing foe to flee for their immortal soul lest it be cast into the fiery pit with the dark one.

The white rat refused to remove his gaze from the Xhosa man who was captivated by a combination of yellow leopard orchid and beautiful black eagle.

The intoxicated tribesman lost his grip as the eagle fluttered away to rest on her perch, in her master's wagon.

The devious black man, though not half as cunning as our San slave, his eyes followed her fine form, Arnou's figure hugging dress betrayed forbidden thigh, crop top freeing outstretched sleek melanin wings. Water ran down the amazing avian as she settled beside her master's seat. Soepenberg raised his hand to lash the fellow once more yet the rat's tail was brought to a stop by a growling night leopard, "Enough Mr Soepenberg. This is a funeral and the Lord doth bear witness to maltreatment of his children!"

The brutish Boer relented while an enchanted Xhosa awoke, shuffling to the wagon's rear.

Soepenberg addressed Reverend Dower, "My apologies Reverend but if I don't keep them under control who will?"

"Perhaps if you brought them to church, I might spread the word and teach them the error of their ways …" he looked Soepenberg up and down, "and you might learn to ease that hand in the process."

Soepenberg made the tiniest of sneers, "What's God ever done for me? He's taken my wife, even the bastaards won't work for me after what happened in Cape Town."

"And you hold the Almighty accountable for your misdeeds?"

"Well, I didn't kill my wife did I?"

"Perhaps if you were present at your farm rather than conducting the Devil's choir in Cape Town you would have both your wife and your Griqua staff?"

Another man and Soepenberg would've taken the whip hand to him but this was Reverend Dower, Pastor of Kokstad. To employ violence on the Reverend in exchange for moral correction would have placed Adam Kok III in a difficult position, he'd begged the Reverend to come here, moving Kokstad's location in order that Dower establish a ministry.

No, Soepenberg would once again have the foul end of a corrupt covenant. He lowered the whip hand, there was a communal sigh. The rat looked past Reverend Dower to observe witnesses who'd attended his wife's funeral, they gasped while ogling the interaction.

The rat sneered, "I'll see you another time Reverend."

As Soepenberg left, Reverend Dower replied in a loud voice so all might detect, "May God be with you Mr Soepenberg."

Chapter Nine: Tikoloshe

As an architect might build a structure Adam Kok strategized the coming of a foul storm. Ministers by his side, the bastaard beaver spaced load bearing walls so as to support a roof above their heads. Yet unbeknownst to his counsel their citadel was contrived upon ground that come British rain was likely to transform from hard stone to sandy beach.

During this time Soepenberg planned the running of his farm. Since previous events in Cape Town, namely his failure to kidnap the governor's niece, the devious Dutchman's reputation caused Kokstad's labour pool to run dry, at least where he was concerned.

No Griqua would work his farm after Jan's abandonment to British rope and so the fiendish farmer was left with but one course of action, to promote Xhosa slaves to positions formerly held by Griquas.

The Xhosa are a tribe which populate KwaNatal or "The Natal" as the British call it. This tribe is very similar to the Zulu in so much that should a white man who'd recently disembarked a Bristol steamer observe Zulu and Xhosa alongside, he'd be at a loss to discern any great difference in dress or feature.

To a native of the cape region their separation was stark, for Zulu and Xhosa wore distinctly different colours. The Zulu are noted for multi-coloured bead work, a skill embossing their culture upon not only Africa's societal landscape but on traders across the globe.

Their languages, inseparable to a foreigner, are quite distinct, both Xhosa and Zulu tongue spread far across Africa today.

Imagine if a Zulu or Xhosa were plucked from 1870's Africa and dropped onto the continent of Europe, what difference might he discern between French and Englishman?

Even should one fellow reek of garlic and possess a string of onions around his neck while the other consume a pork pie washed down by a mug of warm bitter, would a Zulu recognise these factors as being indicative of one nation above the other?

When tribes live beside one another they often adopt customs deemed worthy of replication, sworn enemies or not.

The Xhosa, like the French, were very different or at least they consider themselves so. They, like the French were usually at odds with their neighbours, enough so that during the time of Shaka Zulu fire from Shaka's furnace did steel Xhosa skin.

In the past, the Xhosa nation was formed by Shaka Zulu himself, a blunder rather than deliberate action. During Zulu expansion when Shaka hunted trivial tribes across East Africa, absorbing those who fled or failed to resist, there was a Chief named Mthembu.

Like many before him he fled an oncoming impi cyclone and formed the Tembu Kingdom, the kingdom's clans became collectively known as the Xhosa.

And so Xhosa and Zulu were forged by hatred and malevolence, two separate clans yet inextricably welded together.

The Devil made these pair brothers, remaining at one another's throats through the centuries. Since the 19th century until now violence has made its way to the streets of South Africa, Xhosa and Zulu fighting over a feud more than 200 years old, a feud that to any sane individual has absolutely no bearing on the real world.

Yet men are fools, fools then, fools today and since past is prologue they will be fools tomorrow, yet the greater fool is he who ventures between these tribal differences, no, it is best to allow this estranged family to fight it out amongst themselves until a victor is declared, rather than risk your own neck for a bunch of worthless natives ... at least that was the white rat's reasoning.

So now you understand why Soepenberg had no Zulu slaves working his fields. Better to own Xhosa or Zulu, or neither and stick with Indian and Malay slaves.

For to have both Xhosa and Zulu on one's farm, even as slaves, was detrimental to a man's investment. Before now owners had been killed and establishments burnt to the ground, for when Xhosa and Zulu clashed death became a certainty and at best a Boer would lose his assets in the form of dead slaves, at worst, a pile of ashes where his farm once stood.

So the blonde Boer gathered his least lazy Xhosa and gave them positions of authority, better food and less work.

Soepenberg made it their responsibility to drive others to fields, day in day out, ploughing, seeding, tending and harvesting plants.

Virginia and Oriental tobaccos are harvested leaf by leaf, but Soepenberg's farm grew Burley tobacco, allowing the whole plant to be harvested then air cured in barn.

Amongst these men walked a young fellow, the man who that past week had drawn scent from Arnou's leopard orchid into his body.

His eyes still smouldered with passion, he knew not what they sought, yet he sensed a yearning within and each time he caught a glimpse of the eagle his loins did stir.

One Saturday afternoon while Soepenberg took a horse and surveyed his estate, looking for damage, whether that be crops or fencing, Arnou worked the kitchens preparing supper, a sugar bean soup.

This soup is essentially a beef chuck and onion soup, with sugar beans, ingredients easily come by in Griqualand.

Aunty observed as Arnou added Worcestershire sauce, her keen eye monitoring a young San preparing one of her master's favourites.

"Not too much, you'll drown out the pepper!" snapped Aunty, for this soup is a tricky balance of flavours that only come together in the last 10 minutes of cooking, if one is too dominant it will kill its compatriots, spoiling the harmony of an orchestra of ingredients.

"Yes Aunty," replied Arnou with a smile.

"If kitchen work pleases you so perhaps you would like to wash the dishes?" stated the old cook.

Arnou giggled to herself as she put the sauce down and returned to stirring soft beans, beef and onion.

One of Aunty's eyes widened, usually a horrifying sight yet it had no effect on the eagle's demeanour, "That Xhosa fool, he's caught your eye hasn't he?"

"No Aunty," rebuked the black eagle, her demeanour changing rapidly.

"He has an eye for you child, be warned of his type, Xhosa are only one step away from Zulu!"

Arnou laughed, "I don't care for Xhosa or Zulu."

"Yet he cares for you, bah, these Xhosa, they are a cob stripped of maze in an ashen pit!"

Now the proverb, "Ngumpa wezala," or in English, "It is a cob stripped of maize in an ash pit," is a Xhosa phrase used to denote an individual's worthless nature.

Aunty had a low opinion of Xhosa, for what reason? Who knows? Perhaps it was due to her being San?

Arnou grinned as she stirred the pot, "Master Soepenberg set him straight," the young girl exuded an extra warm smile.

Aunty noted our San slave glow as the morning sun, the old maid was alarmed, "When a hippo eats a cactus, it trusts its anus!"

The young girls working the kitchen burst out laughing, for the proverb was not intended as a joke yet they took it in a different manner.

Its meaning is to warn others not to imitate something they have no capacity for, yet Arnou had little concern for the truth nestled within this idiom and instead, like the young ladies working the kitchen, decided to have a chuckle.

Aunty shook her head for it seemed impossible to change Arnou's thoughts, "Uyakuva into embi eyaviwa ngu Hili wase Mambalwini," stated the old round maid, shifting her eye back to making a pastry.

Another idiom that in direct translation means, "You will find out what Hili of the Amambalu experienced."

Another warning, for Hili or Tikoloshe is a common character in folklore across South Africa, a mischievous dwarf like spirit that lives in water.

The tikoloshe can vary, from a sprite that scares children to a fully-fledged demon, summoned by an umthakathi, a sorcerer, but the sorcerer who worships and raises spirits is specifically referred to as a 'Tikoloshe man'.

If the witch doctor is evil he often sells vengeance, taking the soul of a loved one in exchange for terrorising the client's target.

An evil sorcerer enchants a corpse with magical powder and spikes its eyes with a hot rod penetrating its brain. The tikoloshe will possess said cadaver and begin its reign of terror.

This zombie will create mayhem and death for the victim and once through with his work, perhaps years later, will take the soul of one of the client's family member, whichever one the tikoloshe is most inclined to at the time.

At its least dangerous the tikoloshe will go around and milk cows, take human form and cause women to fall in love with it, or frighten children.

Nevertheless, the proverb is intended as a warning, behave yourself lest the tikoloshe punish you.

The evil spirit might be banished by a Pastor and so Griquas take the requirement for a church and resident holy man seriously. Not all believe in the tikoloshe but it is a commonly held belief amongst Xhosa, Zulu and Khoi-San. The only thing slaves fear more than the whip is the tikoloshe man and an evil umthakathi.

The girls stopped giggling, for mere mention of such evil generated disquiet, "Aunty," stated Arnou in a soft tone as if the tikoloshe man were listening, "be careful."

The old maid sneered, "You've been seeing the Sangoma, haven't you?"

"Who told you that nonsense?" snapped Arnou returning her attention to the soup, doing her utmost to end this conversation.

Aunty whispered so only she and Arnou could hear her words, "I have seen her, on this farm."

Arnou's wide eyes locked onto her wonky eyed superior, "I don't know what you're talking about."

"Don't lie to me child but listen instead, she is no sangoma … she is umthakathi, she does not speak to ancestors but congregates with tikoloshe … some say she is tikoloshe herself!"

Arnou was grabbed by fright, the eagle's claw slipped dropping her spoon to the floor, terror grasped her body for now she understood how and why … it was not her imagination but she'd been manipulated by a dealer in the dead, a sorcerer who traded human souls … an evil spirit.

The metal instrument sent a clang throughout the kitchen pulling everyone's attention into the eye of its storm, as a black hole might draw in matter and energy, crushing it forever.

"Leave girls, I have this now," stated Aunty.

Two girls quickly exited the kitchen leaving Arnou trapped in fright as if a giant cobra had leapt from tall grass, opened its mighty hood and let a terrifying hiss escape.

What the eagle failed to understand at this moment was Aunty's meaning, for she had lived many years and was quite conscious of the tikoloshe man.

Before Arnou or Soepenberg had settled outside Kokstad, before the Reverend Dower founded his church, there was another ministry thriving amongst the slave community.

A tikoloshe man was feared and revered, he bartered in vengeance causing mayhem amongst Zulu, Xhosa and Khoi-San alike.

On this issue the Xhosa and Zulu did put all hatred behind one another ... they must get rid of the tikoloshe man ... but how?

For he did congregate both night and day with evil spirits and should you turn on him, he possessed the power to unleash a tikoloshe. Any man or woman that dared come up against the tikoloshe man would most certainly be cursed by evil.

A Pastor might banish the evil spirit he controlled, yet no such man was present.

Xhosa and Zulu placed differences aside and formed a pact, a scheme as cunning as the tikoloshe man himself.

One of the Zulu knew this tikoloshe man from many years past, he'd terrorised a village until they paid a missionary to bless their land, expelling his demons, yet no such holy man was available in Kokstad.

The beleaguered community were aware of a Zulu woman who knew something of this sorcerer's heritage and so they put what little they could scrape together and sent for her.

She was shocked to discover Zulu and Xhosa working side by side, not a harsh word spoken between them.

In today's day and age, if one were from a European country one might celebrate such a situation with joy, this Zulu did not share the naivety of today's white women, she understood evil had come upon this community, she sensed it as if a Grootslang did stalk these lands, for only fear might bring these tribes together, why, even the British Army wasn't nearly so fearsome to these tribes.

For clarification, the Grootslang is an Afrikaans word which translates into English as "Great Snake."

The monster lives in a cave known to local inhabitants as "The Wonder Hole" in the Richtersveld area of South Africa.

The first Grootslang was too powerful so in fear the Gods cut it into two pieces, these became the elephant species and the snake species.

That being so, one or two Grootslang escaped the Gods by hiding beneath ground, and distanced from fate they reproduced.

This monster can grow up to 60 feet long and 3 feet wide, has four tusks, two horns and a spiked tail. It looks more like an elephant than a serpent yet is a combination of the two.

According to African mythology its cave is full of diamonds yet none can say for certain since the Grootslang has killed and eaten every man, woman and child that did venture close enough to its home.

So, this Zulu female was shook and then when asked to approach the tikoloshe man and purchase vengeance she refused.

The payment was doubled, and doubled again, and finally she did accept.

You see the tikoloshe will take the soul of your intended victim in exchange for a member of your family, what the tikoloshe man didn't know, but the tikoloshe did, was that this lady was the tikoloshe man's only surviving relative.

And so they targeted a Boer, a man particularly handy with the whip, the tikoloshe killed him, then a year or so later it took the tikoloshe man.

The Zulu and Xhosa were freed from his reign of spiritual terror ... until the day came to clear out the tikoloshe man's hut and they found an old lady had moved in, an old lady who'd died the same day as the tikoloshe man. While they cremated the tikoloshe man and celebrated with drum and umqombothi, her corpse rose from its deathbed, made its way into the tikoloshe man's hut and set up residence.

Had the tikoloshe man's soul used her recently expired corpse, reanimating it so he might continue his reign of terror? Or was this a miracle?

The old woman's family confirmed the situation; it was not their grandmother but a demon infesting her body. Word quickly spread as bad news often does, and they'd come to the conclusion that the tikoloshe man was not only back but out for vengeance, yet it refrained from using the spirits directly on those it wished to punish, rather it would dupe the foolish into cursing members of the community and their own family, while he/she/it pretended to be a sangoma. There was the added factor that in order to sustain its revival from the after world, the tikoloshe man must consume the spirits of the living so it might pay the Devil his tithe for a second lease of what some might describe as life ... the entire community agreed that the sorcerer had become tikoloshe himself. Had the tikoloshe man's spirit come for revenge and if so who was its target? Nevertheless Kokstad's locals had celebrated the tikoloshe man's passing prematurely and they required a Pastor to bless this community in order they chase out its evil spirit and so they set about influencing the Griqua administration.

This is why Reverend Dower's seemingly outrageous demands were met, yet the sangoma travelled with them to the current site of Kokstad. Fortunately the Pastor's presence kept its evil leashed, to a degree.

And so the truth became clear to Arnou, she'd purchased not a sangoma's sage advice but roused tikoloshe vitriol. The San woman was destined to a terrible end, for anyone who dealt with the tikoloshe man did deal in darkness, bargaining with base ancient evil that undoubtedly wished to consume her soul.

Arnou locked her eyes with the wonky vision of Aunty, tears formed as dams on the brink of spilling over, "Help me Aunty," she whispered.

Aunty, as wide as she was tall, shook her head in regret, for once you begin to dance with the tikoloshe, no-one, man, woman or beast might cut in and divert you from its turbid jig.

"Please," petitioned the eagle, yet the staunch servant refused to budge, not that she had any choice.

"You must dance this dance on your own child, you have chosen to take the path of evil and so it will overtake you the moment you miss a step, I am sorry," replied the old maid in a pitiful tone.

"What might I do Aunty, to stay ahead of the tikoloshe?" The old woman made a mighty huff as she eyed the trembling slave from top to bottom and back with her odd eye, "Bah, even the tikoloshe man could not see his destiny, his soul was consumed by the evil he conjured. No child, you have done the same as he, you've had dealings with a demon, allowing it to delve within your mind collecting all that is evil, using your desire for its own wicked purpose."

Arnou's dams began to overflow with salt water, flooding melanin valleys beneath before streaking onto canoe like lips until flood waters roared over a cliff face that is Arnou's chin.

Aunty had not witnessed Arnou shed tears before now, for she was a strong woman who kept her feminine weakness hidden from the outside world, managing her emotions by strength of will, yet today she lost control.

"Perhaps you have a family member here and the tikoloshe will take them?"

"No, my family died on the Great Trek, I am the only one left," she wept, clearing her eyes as Aunty looked on with disdain.

"Then your fate is set in stone, the tikoloshe will come for you."

"Help me Aunty, how might I protect my soul from a circling succubus?"

Aunty's big round head shook as her odd eye maintained its fix on the eagle, "If I knew that, I would be the wealthiest woman in Africa and the white man would serve my supper."

The San slave wailed out loud, expending all commiseration for the miserable bed she'd made herself, stepping into the path of a tikoloshe, an African demon which consumes the souls of mortal men and women, all in the hope she'd take the place of Hannah and become lady of the house.

After bleating her hindmost heart ache, like a lamb lost in the snow, the harsh reality of winter overtaking slight warmth, the catastrophe at hand blew out a pilot light of regret with an arctic blast assaulting our black beauty's bones.

Sensing a creeping chill from somewhere beyond the kitchen space Arnou peered with trepidation toward its origin … her heart was frozen hard as ice atop Mt Kilimanjaro.

Our beautiful eagle had been forced to roost high on the peaks of Africa's tallest point, the three peaks of Kilimanjaro were obvious, the shortest, foolhardiness, Shira. Next pushing from dense cloud obscuring lands below was desire, or better known as peak Mawenzi. Both of these peaks are dormant stratovolcanos, however the third, upon which she nested, was the highest peak, Kibo or better known as despair.

Here Arnou stiffened, her wings beaten by freezing winds of fate, for our eagle saw a dark figure lurking outside the kitchen window, it was difficult to make out yet the cold in her soul did identify a pitch black crone.

The sangoma approached, she knew not how for Arnou did not witness her walk as a human might, no, it seemed to Arnou that her vision did focus, bringing a zombified corpse closer to her sensibilities, or was the tikoloshe grabbing her faculties and shifting them through a desolate atmosphere towards her? At times such as these, when a man is dying in freezing cold, his senses become most acute.

The old crone's opaque eyes sparkled as its inner demon frolicked in the misery beating down upon our eagle.

Aunty followed Arnou's vision and jumped, "It is here, the tikoloshe is close at hand my child!"

"Help me," whispered the eagle, barely able to muster a sound while hardening onto Mt Kilimanjaro's glacier.

"It is too late my child, you have made your bargain with the Devil and he will take his toll."

The tikoloshe vanished into a cloud of vapour as a Xhosa slave walked past, the tribesman, oblivious to the tikoloshe's presence, made an odd expression while he sniffed atmosphere, a stench of sulphur filled widening nostrils as they flexed on an odd breeze. The slave halted, then looked around before noticing Arnou … it was the same man who'd taken to her after absorbing the love potion, he smiled at the eagle, the hawk sneered back, a voice called out and the Xhosa fellow moved away, never cutting his sordid stare from our beauty, standing beside a kitchen stove flanked by Aunty.

Aunty grabbed Arnou's shoulders, "You must go to Reverend Dower, he might expel the demons you've unleashed on this household."

The chill subsided and Arnou awoke as a bear from its cave, the African slave's brain allowed Aunty's advice to defrost a crippling winter chill.

While warming back into the kitchen's environment she thought for a moment before nodding her head, "Yes, Reverend Dower, he is my only hope now."

Chapter Ten: Xhosa Slain

Soepenberg enacted his evening ritual, a supper of soup and bread before retiring to the porch. The rat lit a bowl of African shag in a briar pipe purchased during his Cape Town escapade. Briar being a wood traditionally used in pipes during these times and since; however, outside areas of major trade and industry, you'd often find it substituted by local ferns.

When the Dutch initially appeared on the Cape they smoked clay pipes, cheap to make, easily disposed of and replaced, they were common. Why, even today, should you venture into the mud of the River Thames at low tide, you're guaranteed to find an assortment of clay corpses littering its banks, tobacco pipes from the 16th to 19th century.

The Cape has its own traditions, previously men smoked cannabis, better known as "dagga", in a water pipe long before the white man brought tobacco.

By the early 20th century the clay pipe was no longer in production, totally replaced by its stalwart briar brother, a wood extracted from a short shrub which grows mainly around the Mediterranean.

Its properties permit the smoker to grasp its bowl or any part of its exterior while smoking his leaf.

Unlike clay pipes briar is highly resistant to heat. This is why you'll see many old pictures or photographs depicting a man holding his clay pipe by the stem, close to where smoke exits into his mouth.

Clay pipes were still common in pubs and inns throughout Christendom, yet as a man of means Soepenberg had decided to invest in an imported Italian briar.

A simple brown pipe, smooth with a tobacco stained ivory bit for its mouthpiece. It was by far superior to its clay cousins littering the streets and harbours of every British port in the Cape Colony and beyond.

He relaxed in typical attire, thick leather work boots, trousers made of the same thick brown material, a thick yellow cotton shirt and leather outback hat.

Sitting in his chair, the sun fell beneath Africa's wide horizon, broad as its people's shoulders, while his bowl of shag laboured under a match, smoke ascended, polluting atmosphere above his hat.

Slaves had been sent to their separate lodges and locked away.

San house slaves slept in their own quarters attached to the master's residence.

Soepenberg observed Helios drive his chariot beneath luscious land while contemplating the disastrous month gone by. He'd failed in a plot to keep the British at bay.

The rat's actions had in fact accelerated Anglo-Saxon foreboding while abandoning Griqua workers to British rope; another man might have called Jan his friend but the white rat kept a distance from men.

Some, like Reverend Dower, trusted in God. Some, like Adam Kok III, trusted in men. Some, such as Arnou, trusted in the ancestors. Soepenberg trusted in nought but his own devilish cunning, his ability to usurp others and in doing so this Afrikaner did bypass God ... so far it'd done him proud. However, since the catastrophe of Cape Town the blonde Boer began to pay the piper in lieu of past evils so calmly committed.

Like the outside of his pipe, the loathsome and unscrupulous had become smooth and even, slipping from tongue before resting within hand, softening a cantankerous conscience and so granting ease in treachery, theft and even murder.

Soepenberg's purpose always furthered by the rancorous and foul, until recently, for now fate was reborn, a tikoloshe did roam his lands searching out souls as a cheetah doth hunt game on plains, running down its target until exhaustion overtakes its victim's frame, consuming its prey's life force, mocking the foolish non-believer, face stained red with hot blood while dining on human innards.

All this was taking place in the immediate vicinity of the white rat yet he remained oblivious, his negligence stretched so wide as to encompass him and his wife, yet she rested in heaven while he would be set within the depths of hell, where another demon prepared to cavort upon his miserable soul, frolicking as flames flicker upon his immortal being, never to die ... never to love, laugh or truly live again but always to mourn his miscalculation ... yet none would hearken his cry, for the choir of torment doth drown out individual chanter.

This had yet to pass, for Soepenberg's destiny here in Africa was greater than he could imagine, for he is merely a cog in the machine of God, as are we all, some larger than others, many small such as Soepenberg, moving quickly so as to moderate the calm rotation of larger wheels noted in our history books.

For great events are to take place South Africa, historic cogs set on beautiful jewels transmitting a story upon the face of time, each incident requiring many small greasy wheels to keep the tale in motion. This is why God doth tolerate these foul mechanisms, hidden behind gears and tusks, permitting them operation despite the wonderment of good men who often query in their minds as to why the Lord permit these terrors prosper, consenting to their circumvention of justice.

Little do they know that once that moving part has served its purpose, our Lord and Saviour Jesus Christ doth pluck him from his father's mechanism before casting him into the furnace that is Hell where his soul shall melt away, merging with pain and torture for eternity.

If permitted a mere glimpse of these places every man and woman reading this would amend their ways, no matter how small, for we are all sinners to one degree or another, those who request forgiveness from the Lord shall be saved, but miscreants, such as the white rat, shall be skinned alive and roasted on Beelzebub's barbecue.

As Soepenberg whiled away a clement evening, pipe in one hand, heavy heart in the other, Arnou was going about cleaning duties.

As was her habit she prepared the now deceased lady of the house's bedchamber. After her passing, Hannah's bed sheets had been used to sew her body into a cocoon before she was cast within a lime pit.

Airing new sheets each day was one of many duties entrusted to our San slave. As she spread linen over a brand new hair mattress, a door opened to her rear. At first the eagle failed to detect its activity until a tiny creak alerted her to someone's presence. Assuming it to be Aunty or one of the serving girls Arnou spoke out, but no reply was forthcoming. Concluding drafts within the house had caused the bedchamber door to grind open she continued her work.

Unbeknownst to Arnou a cog in the Devil's machine crept through the open doorway, his eyes smouldering with passion as fiery sun escorting dusk onto African savannah. Influenced by leopard orchid juice, the Xhosa slave, in his early twenties, gawped silently at her firm frame, legs astride as taught arms flicked white linen in the air.

As with all men, strong in fortitude of body and will, above that of any woman, his mind was weak when confronted with the feminine form, unable to resist its scintillating shape.

The burly Xhosa wrestled with an image of beauty positioned before him, although unable to witness the face of her clock his base cunning did tell the time of this seductive San slave, craving her curves his vision flickered upon her hips, dancing upon vibrant flesh while the Devil pressed wicked thoughts as Soepenberg might drive a lazy slave into field, lashing the slave's back, forcing him to obey his master's corrupt inclination.

In this area a woman is superior to her masculine counterpart, for a lady holds an air of superiority when she refrains from lustful behaviour; to which the male has no option but to respect her feminine self-restraint. Unable to subdue himself the tall and powerful Xhosa moved silently, our eagle unaware of his stealth, he slithered in as a snake and then … his foot pressed on a floorboard *CREAK*

Arnou spun around, holding a pillowcase before her body, "What are you doing here?" she spat in Xhosa.

Her question went unanswered, at least with words for his expression was more than enough to transmit intent.

A seedy feeling crawled beneath the skin of our San servant then fear as he continued to approach, the Devil in his eyes, twinkling with a mania endowed by the tikoloshe, facilitated by leopard orchid, with but a single purpose governing his mind, body and soul.

"Leave this place, go back to your hut, NOW!" shouted Arnou, her voice losing pitch in fear of what might pass. She hoped Aunty or a kitchen girl might detect her alarm … they did not, and so the Xhosa proceeded toward his goal, grasped the linen pillowcase and tossed it aside, his vision firmly fastened to Arnou's frame at all times.

The Xhosa, no longer a slave to Soepenberg but to the forces of evil gawped at our ebony avian, a snake, famished of feminine contact, ravening the refinement of tender female form, driven by the Devil while tempted by a tikoloshe, he could no longer resist and so beauty and beast clashed. He clutched her by the arms, she cried out, he failed to hearken her howl, the dark demon drooled, saliva dripped down his lips for the union of the snake and eagle drove his mind into a mania directing his body with wickedness so as to satisfy this evil concoction.

He pressed her body against his, forcing his slobbering lips upon hers, vile vinegar violating sweet African honey. She tried to break his grip yet years of hard labour endowed this fiend with the body of a powerful man, there would be no warding off his demonic will.

This manic Xhosa's powerful hand flexing in the dawn of Helios moved down and gripped her rear, a thick taught African hind few men, white or black are able to refute, for its unique arrangement doth send normal human beings, architects, politicians, store keepers, sailors and slaves alike into a stupor.

In moments he would strip his prey and consume her defenceless body. He pulled away for a moment, the visage of a fiend peered back at Arnou, a sight of terror, for through his eyes this Xhosa's mind was plain to see, its cogs spun in a madness, gathering insanity as they travelled quicker and quicker.

The Xhosa slave smiled at his prize, for she was his, his soul mate, a beautiful woman fused to his craving via the magic of leopard orchid.

As he smiled Arnou was about to scream yet before releasing her squawk, a thunderous crack filled the room, perhaps lightning had struck the farm while the tikoloshe watched on? Laughing with the Devil over rape and ruination?

But no, there was no lightning, for half a second later the Xhosa lost his self-satisfied grin, his face drained as a cracked dam might reveal a dark dirty river bed of horrifying rocks waiting to cause pain and misery to all who venture too deep.

His pain and fear exposed, a second deafening crack followed the first in short order to which strength abandoned his body. Arnou sensed his grip crumble as an old hut in hard rain and so she slipped from his grasp. Moving out of the Xhosa's hold Arnou observed Soepenberg at the bedroom door, whip in hand.

"Get back to your hut kaffir!" bellowed the white rat, hatred and fury breaking the skin of an enchanted Xhosa. The black slave spun around … due to a combination of leopard orchid, Arnou's stunning beauty, the influence of a tikoloshe and years of pent up anger towards the white man … his time was at hand.

Thinking with the urgency of youth obscured within a cloud of passion, for desire of the soft and supple woman is only a step away from the hard brutality of revenge, much as two horses tied alongside each other at a hitching post outside a drinking tavern. If one equine takes task to cause a ruckus and pull free, so his brother will follow, for they are two emotions kept in check by the experience of age and wisdom.

So both stallions did kick and tug, tearing down a post to which they'd been tied for so long. The post crumbled and reins fell free as legs kicked and emotions neighed, unaware of imposing danger these stallions kicked dust in a crazed contest over a beautiful black mare.

The Xhosa colt cared not, all it saw in its polluted mind was a white rat blocking his path toward the receptacle of his seed.

He discarded pain, moving on an ivory cad who'd governed his vitality for so long, he displayed African intent to beat this vermin to death with brute fists.

Soepenberg observed a Xhosa slave elevate himself, for he wished to kill his owner; in the Xhosa's mind the white man was degraded to no more than vermin he would squash under hoof, for all men occupy the same excrement filled trench flowing through this slave's mind, all are driven insane by the beauty of the black woman and the evil of the African spirit world.

Reinvigorated by African evil and black magic the Xhosa moved on his master, murder his intent, eyes of a fiend, ready to dispose of human life for the smallest pipe of opium, yet his opium was sexual desire and revenge.

Soepenberg witnessed fire in a slave's eyes as he enlarged both physically and spiritually, the rat had acted to save his San servant yet self-defence was now at hand and in such a situation Soepenberg would sacrifice anyone and anything for he was vermin, a vile gutter snipe feeding off rotten African dead.

Soepenberg cracked his whip before the Xhosa, something like a cobra standing up from the long grass while opening its hood and hissing ... it had no effect.

He lashed the whip around the slave's throat pulling it taught, yet this action served only to draw him closer and so the young black man swung his fists.

Soepenberg blocked a strike to his head but a hook cracked his ribcage forcing the slave owner's lungs to evacuate. Pain rippled through Soepenberg's body, physically and mentally, he'd not experienced a slave with the audacity to assault his master, for the punishment would be either the whipping post or death.

Soepenberg was not inclined to kill a man, not because it was immoral but due to the financial loss incurred, the rat expected a return when investing in Xhosa slaves. Killing slaves would be no different than burning his crop of burley tobacco yet this man continued in reckless violence while Soepenberg's pain intensified alongside Arnou's scream. Aunty and the San girls appeared at the door, adding to a chorus of wails as their master was beaten down, his whip useless at such close quarters.

It seemed that Soepenberg's demise approached yet Arnou's quick mind directed her limbs and she darted to the fireplace, picked up a fire iron which had gone unused since lady Hannah's passing.

The fire iron, a long heavy poker with a large iron barb at one end and brass handle at the other, might be employed as a formidable weapon.

"MASTER!" shrieked Arnou as she slipped her hand beneath Xhosa fists pounding a white rat into the ground.

Soepenberg peered up with a look of desperation he grabbed the fire poker. Upon taking this piece of grey, ashen metal, he let go of his leather whip replacing it with sturdy iron.

Standing up with renewed resolution, emboldened by the Devil, inspired by tikoloshe and fuelled by retribution he lifted the iron above his head, Aunty and her girls gasped before a bruised and bloodied rat brought it down, cracking his slave's skull as an overripe water melon.

At that the Xhosa halted, iron from the gods splitting mortal skull asunder, clearing his thoughts to what had transpired, momentarily the Xhosa was taken by the realization that desire had dictated his downfall for but a single San slave.

His face, one of utter shock hung from his body as a painting from a wall, suspended in mid-air, unable to move but for a swing so he might view Arnou one last time.

His vision locked with hers while releasing his final utterance as bubbles reaching the surface of a cauldron full of blood and saliva ... "Murderer .... you ... you ... you murdered the mute swan ..."

Aunty's odd eye expanded somewhat greater than the other, increasing in size to scrutinise our San slave, the girls quietened down in wonder.

It is said that when crossing that barrier between life and death, the demesne which maintains balance lest one domain creep into the other, many truths are revealed, concerning past, present and future.

For what we call prophecy the Africans of this region do achieve by communion with their ancestors, harkening the words of the dead, and so it is understood that this Xhosa, as he passed into the night only gods, demons and angels may return from, did witness a kernel of truth pertinent to the living.

Was Arnou to murder, be murdered or had she murdered? And who did he witness that resembles a mute swan?

Already the staff sifted their brains to discover a single grain of enlightenment marking the path of truth in a dark jungle of ignorance.

Meanwhile Soepenberg focused on dispatching his attacker, he was unconcerned by sooth saying and metaphors for he was a sceptic when considering Christianity … let alone backward African beliefs.

Striking downwards with a second blow harder than the first, thick dark blood bubbled as a well spring; the slave's skull opened as crocodile's jaws to reveal beating brains, the girls shrieked, Aunty and Arnou remained silent while observing a Xhosa fool's tortuous death.

For Aunty understood his divination while Arnou urged the Xhosa's passing, before he might betray further information concerning the evil she'd committed in this very room. It were as if the spirit of Soepenberg's wife haunted her old bedchamber infusing her will onto a dying Xhosa during his final moments, in an effort to transmit a message of warning to her husband and convict Arnou's evil acts, yet Hannah was unsuccessful for her husband was not impressed by the primitive beliefs of simpletons.

The possessed slave lost strength in his legs and collapsed to the floor; where young vitality once stood now dwelled a crumpled bloody mess.

Everyone sighed with relief, save two people, for they alone did witness the tikoloshe; for as the Xhosa slumped he revealed the old woman, or at least her image, directly behind, directing his actions as a puppet master.

Aunty drew a deep breath, with one eye fixed on the tikoloshe and the other upon Arnou. Arnou screamed in horror, an evil grin beamed as the old crone delighted in the eagle's terror.

A beaten and bloody Soepenberg stood over collapsed Xhosa, his senses obscured in an adrenaline fuelled haze, breathing heavily after much exertion; fire iron pointed downwards, pattering thick African blood upon floor below.

Arnou screeched as a hawk attempting to scare hyenas away from its fallen chick, all the time steam silently rose not only from Soepenberg's back but a dead Xhosa's wounds.

Aunty and Arnou witnessed an odd viscous gas exit the Xhosa's split skull as he passed into the afterlife … it seemed to bear the makings of thought as if alive rather than an inert substance such as steam, which strictly obeys the laws of physics so permitting its future path to be wholly predictable.

This substance, which only Arnou and Aunty witnessed, moved upwards making its way to the Tikoloshe. The vile spirit opened its mouth and consumed the gas, which Arnou recognised as the spirit of a man whose life had been taken, first by Soepenberg and now by a tikoloshe. The Xhosa would join the others, as slaves corralled by their master, forced to do his bidding, punished on a demonic whim.

Once the Xhosa's soul had been consumed the creature let go one final grin, mocking its client before vanishing in a fizzle of dark smoke, leaving behind a stench vultures are most familiar with, before swooping upon a rotten corpse exposed upon savannah.

At that moment our San slave did halt her cries. Aunty sniffed the air, taking note of the tikoloshe's customary stench.

"Get this dirty kaffir out of here," stated Soepenberg to the girls while he turned to Arnou, "Come with me," he instructed our black eagle as he led her from the bedroom.

Chapter Eleven: The Bed Chamber

Master and menials retired alongside Hyperion as he slipped beneath primitive horizon, illuminating Selene in African night sky.

Selene, sister of Helios and Eos, lover of Endymion …

Endymion formerly King of Elis, a budding man sent into an unending sleep by his lover so she may enjoy his endless youth undisturbed.

Even today he sleeps in eternity, Selene making love to him at night, it is said she bore him 50 children. Blessed and cursed by his relationship with the Gods, for he will never die, never grow old yet neither is he to taste the fruits of such a bounty.

As Selene took control of night another goddess made herself known to all, Modjadji, literally 'Rain Queen'.

She comes from a line of Queens of the Balobedu people in South Africa. Balobedu, or in English 'The mineral miners' being one of the oldest civilizations in the region, it is said their Queens control rainfall.

Even today a council is held to ordain their next Modjadji or 'Rain Queen'.

This evening Modjadji could be heard tapping on the roof, gathering pace, mimicking an endless sack of lentils poured upon a kitchen table.

Outside, in the courtyard beside the whipping post, a white cocoon smeared with black blood absorbed the Rain Queen's purity, washing away foul indiscretion while mud swirled around its base, tainting white linen with reddish clay.

Amidst the deluge, Arnou rose while Aunty snored yet the noise of Modjadji drowned her out. One of the girls was still awake, yet on meeting the eagle's glare she returned to slumber.

Our San slave carefully closed the door to the staffs' quarters and slipped into dark without an oil lamp to guide her way.

Travelling the house Arnou made her way into her master's bedchamber. He lay in work clothes, bloodied and bruised from his prior altercation. Neither hour nor climate permitted a visit from Doctor Albronda, not until the following day, and even then Modajadji might block his path.

With no wife to tend his wounds Soepenberg lay in a restless state, attempting to join Endymion, for there is more than a single tale as to how he ended up in that cave. One account describes how Zeus offered him anything he might desire and so Endymion requested eternal youth and everlasting sleep.

At this moment Soepenberg would have been satisfied with everlasting sleep.

Arnou crept within, Selene's light beamed into the room for tonight's moon was full and her sleek onyx skin reflected its glow, alerting the white rat to another's presence.

He flinched, immediately grabbing the fire iron, a mixture of blood and ash stained its tip.

Arnou jumped but uttered no noise, for fear she might wake Aunty and scupper her scheme.

"Master, it is I, Arnou."

Soepenberg tried to focus yet one of his eyes had puffed to the point it obscured his sight. Despite Selene's illumination the bruised rat failed to properly discern his slave from the dark.

"Come closer, slowly," whispered Soepenberg as rain beat down.

The eagle approached revealing itself to the white rat.

"What do you want?" inquired Soepenberg in a raspy voice.

"I came to tend your wounds master," replied Arnou in a fragile tone.

Arnou produced a rag from her hip pouch, there was a bowl of fresh water on his bedside and she began to dab his wounds.

As she tended his eye the blonde Boer detected the scent of leopard lotus. The exact odour which had driven a Xhosa youth wild filled the rat's nostrils.

It was a unique incense, a pheromone contrived by allure and mystery ... he was quickly released from his trauma.

Placing fire iron down, nostrils flared, Soepenberg's olfactory senses danced a tango with African desire.

During this stormy night a blonde and bloodied Boer transformed, from injured rat to hungry hyena, his mouth, dry as dirt encompassing his farm was doused in rains of base lust, transmuting into thick honeyed wine.

The adrenaline of being brought within inches of his life, the thrill of teetering on the edge of existence before pulling back to murder his assailant in a brutal hate fuelled tantrum, that wicked rush returned to his senses. This rat was able to plumb the depths of passion, juxtaposed hours before when Soepenberg was lost in a moment of man to man combat.

Grasping his slave's arms, she halted from tending his body and asked, "Master?"

He tore animal skin from our eagle's top. Arnou's face filled with shock as a mirage might create an oasis in the desert. Seemingly real yet in truth a visual illusion, for beneath lay the cool calculation of a shrewd woman.

For woman, unlike man, does understand the arithmetic of love. She can subtract, divide and find the correct solution no matter how abstract the equation may seem … to a man.

Her dark breasts shook with tremors of penned passion, the rat cast his slave down with force, her face maintained quiet shock, fighting to prevent a San smile of satisfaction from surfacing and so betray her true intentions.

The blonde beast's swollen hands unbuttoned his shirt, so swollen that only moments ago he was unable to carry out the simplest of tasks and so slept in dirty clothes; yet his body became invigorated by the same spirit with which he fought earlier that day; a different flavour of adrenaline pumped through his veins but it was adrenaline nonetheless.

Inflammation vanished from the beast's hands via the black magic of a woman's beauty. Soepenberg's puffed persona transformed, his bewitched eye opened up and permitting sight, while another area of this vile beast's anatomy did the opposite, enlarging the front of this dirty animal's leather pants.

Arnou's eagle eyes danced with delight, her naïve intellect enraptured in every aspect of Soepenberg's revival from beaten and tired man, unable to perform the most elementary task, to reinvigorated youth, no brute so dangerous he could not bring it to heel.

As Soepenberg removed his shirt and cast it to the floor Arnou's mind celebrated his masculine mutation. She wished to undo his pants and remove the treasure within, just as those who hunted pharaohs and their worldly possessions in the Nile valley, for she'd discovered the path to this King's burial chamber and was soon to be the only woman alive to witness a mighty sarcophagus betray itself, under the light of African moon.

Anat, the Egyptian goddess of fertility gave the couple her blessings, unfortunately the goddess was also known as a great trouble maker, consort of Ba'al, a god worshipped via child sacrifice and sexual deviancy, a diabolical divinity brought down by the followers of our Lord Jesus Christ. Tonight this divine yet dastardly pair did brew bother on South African savannah.

Arnou sat propped against pillows feigning the appearance of a defenceless child, while within a black eagle squawked in approval.

The rat became a hyena, juices thickened in its mouth from mere saliva into a lusty liqueur. Unable to bridal his desire this wild dog undid its pants much to the eagle's glee.

As Soepenberg's waistband slipped away thick cock struck aloft, slapping this beast's hairy belly as Adam Kok III might smash his gavel against a wooden podium, yet this gavel did not return to its point of origin for the tension of Soepenberg's desire took control, led on by the demands of a slave woman.

He stepped out of his pants and moved onto the bed, all the time Arnou's vision grasped his soul in her talons. Their eyes wrestled with one another as two young men on the pantheon at noon, oiled muscles trembling under judgmental gaze of the gods who muttered to one another, unable to turn away for but a second lest they miss the outcome of such an exquisite contest.

At this moment Arnou was forced to betray truth, for while the eagle focused on its prey our slave's mask did slip; on her thick dark lips happiness made its presence known via contrasting black and pink.

Soepenberg stopped, naked above a San slave sandwiched between him and his bed. Her transformation from terrified child to insidious slut ... a scene of insincerity which caused his senses to buck as a defiant colt resisting base desires, obstructing the leopard orchid and its pull, dragging him into depravity and degeneracy ... at that instance the eagle spread her wings wide, animal hide skirt riding upwards, exposing Satan's winking eye.

Soepenberg did not even recall observing that hidden den all men seek, dripping thick with an extract handed down by the gods, a potion designed by the divine that when applied properly doth remedy all masculine woe.

The hyena's vision secured itself to the eagle's eyes, a dark perception sparkling with the passion of youth and expectation of self-improvement, to raise herself from mere kitchen slave to lady of the house.

Inside the hyena's eyes the eagle witnessed hesitation and so spread further ... permitting the scent of woman's most volatile elixir to mix with leopard orchid, sowing his nostrils with seeds of untamed passion, sprouting in his heart, flowering in his loins, yet he was resistant to Arnou's tribal tactics.

Next our slave moved her lips close to his mouth and whispered, "Fuck me King."

And so the hungry hyena's resistance collapsed as a termite hill before a crash of rhino; utterly diminished before the power of a feminine beast stampeding across African plains, all thoughts of defiance crumbled before her superiority.

Our master manipulator slipped her arms around the rear of his head as a blonde beast unleashed upon spread eagle.

His thick trunk parted the opening of Arnou's African cave, made visible only in the moonlight of scrutinizing deities, licking their lips, sampling the delectable passion of base male desire and feminine fulfilment spread upon this banquet of a bed , for it is a fact that women trade sex for intimacy and men trade intimacy for sex yet this strange combination of black slave and white master, thrown together in the toxic cauldron of Griqualand East, on the Eastern cape of Africa, did result in a unique potion even gods cannot resist.

Soepenberg's manhood tentatively pushed Arnou's gates of wonder, sliding within her garden. At first he met resistance, something kept his rod at bay, as the siege of Eshowe where the impi of King Cetshwayo did halt one of the three prongs of a British advance into Zululand.
Colonel Charles Pearson was tasked with pushing his troops into KwaZulu and taking Eshowe, before marching on Ulundi where British forces would converge for the final assault.
Unfortunately the Zulu had anticipated this action and with superior mobility and numbers, pinned his forces in Eshowe for two months.
Pushing out from Eshowe into beautiful Africa, the forces of Soepenberg were barricaded by Arnou's womanly pressure, so he applied greater impetus while his iron poker consolidated its position.
Her vagina's natural resistance excited a starving hyena, he grasped her collar bone, passion concentrated on a single action.

Our spread eagle gazed at her king's grunting visage, pushing within her garden of love so he might pluck its unique pink fruit.

Soepenberg excited our San slave and so her cave walls flowed with viscous fluid assisting the white traveller's course, leading him onto a treasure of elation hidden deep within. As he pulled back our spread eagle's cave clutched onto the snout of the hyena's rod, exposing her pink innards.

The sight of such powerful contrast mixed with the formidable grip of a woman in love, forced even the gods to raise an eyebrow, for this was no common occurrence, even to deities who'd watched mankind for millennia.

The ebony of Africa surrounding pink innards gripping a trunk of European oak withdrawing in anticipation of a second more powerful stroke.

Slave on master, white in black, ebony on blush, few in history had ogled such an exquisite combination.

Divine brows elevated while this mortal man pushed back, the talons of her vagina holding his sceptre in place as an eagle clutching its chick.

Arnou's thick lips widened expressing deepest pleasure, she felt Soepenberg's veins pumping along her tight flesh, manufacturing excitement beyond anything she'd previously experienced ... or would.

As her master pumped she flowed until like the rain beating upon roof, disguising their liaison, she saturated a thick white shaft stoking her dark cavern.

Vaginal restriction eased, our slave's juices slicked her master's path leading to a harder pump, increased pleasure and further saturation until eventually the sheets displayed a large patch indicative of tonight's activities while the scent of taboo clouded atmosphere with intoxicating odour.

Arnou threw her arms back as waves of joy rippled across her body. With extend grin she stared into his open eyes and said "Fuck me my king, fuck me!"

She encouraged the slave master as he pushed and pulled, staring into her face, nostrils filled with an odd combination of leopard orchid and Arnou's vaginal scent, the stench of sex, desire and lust, a lethal mix out here in the middle of nowhere, on a moonlit night, rain beating hard despite it being completely out of season while the gods engaged in divine voyeurism.

In the barn, slaves and staff looked up in wonder, for this weather was an unexpected event. Added to that a full moon, a slain Xhosa slave and beaten white master, this could not be a good sign.

If aware of events unfolding in the master's bedroom they'd be shocked … Aunty would be terrified, for she understood a tikoloshe was at work and the tikoloshe would not stop feeding on souls until its demonic thirst had been quenched.

The community had abated the spirit once but it was back, the tikoloshe man became tikoloshe himself.

Released by a foolish San girl it was on a vengeful rampage, unsatisfied until Kokstad's final soul had been consumed.

Arnou relaxed, head on pillow, arms spanning the mattress she giggled, "Fuck me you white gal-sneaker."

A "gal-sneaker" being a man devoted to seduction. Pushing and pulling above her dark form the master of the house sneered, while one hand held her leg his free hand slapped Arnou's face with some force before Soepenberg replied, "Shut your mouth you dirty black slut!"

Arnou's reaction shocked the hyena while intriguing the gods, for rather than cry out or struggle she did nought but smile.

Observing the slave grin, happy beyond words, it was at that moment Soepenberg realised it was not he who was in control.

He'd spent all these years as master of slaves, their lives resting in the balance of his judgement yet it was at this moment he lost control, not through violent rebellion, not via British emancipation but the smile of an African woman, it was bothersome and beguiling in the same measure.

A seemingly innocent young slave had bewitched him, manipulating Soepenberg into her cave as a lamb led to the abattoir until truth outshone Selene's illumination and beat louder than Modjadji's rain, at this point the gods smiled while nodding to one another, acknowledging an African female's superior cunning.

For woman had overcome man, not by violence but guile. Soepenberg sensed his authority drain, placing his hips squarely behind his rod of authority he slammed into the African witch, yet with each retraction a piece of himself was relinquished.

With greater velocity and stiffening shaft he pressed, sending salacious shockwaves across our slave's body, her frame shaking to the beat of his manhood in a vain quest to recover authority.

Our San slave bit her bottom lip while revelling in the pleasure she now experienced, for not only did his white prick excite the cloak and dagger within her thick cave but the power transfer of owner to slave was as great an aphrodisiac to Arnou as leopard orchid to Soepenberg.

For the first time in her life Arnou held power over the white man and it was as intoxicating as it was unexpected.

He thumped dark vulva with quicken strokes, gathering steam as his firebox of authority fizzled out, "Harder you white devil!" yelped our San slave in a pitch of sheer delight.

Soepenberg slapped his slave again, "Shut your mouth you dirty whore!"

Arnou's lips grew covering the distance beneath lifted cheeks. A large canoe, so elated it became as the cave below, a fat arrow slit bathed in a beautiful contrast of joy exposing a supple pink lining.

The hyena, drained of authority, became a rat once more, each slap resulting only in tribal titillation. The Dark Continent had revealed one of its secrets, the women of Africa, blessed by their ancestors they possess a power which the white man is unable to surmount ... let alone comprehend.

Exquisite beauty, silky skin, enchanting etiquette, it is her breeding that is in fact of the highest calibre, for she is senior to all women. The tribal woman boast's superior finesse in the art of love, her ancestors handing down not only remarkable culture but first class instincts.

The white man is her superior in ingenuity, for he does outclass all in that perspective. Yet the African woman is principal to all in seduction and the ability to overcome her male counterpart via the employment of feminine whiles, ancestral knowledge, cultural blessings and divine beauty.

He who underestimates the African woman is either destined to become a slave to her femininity or cursed to never experience the divine pleasure of possessing a tribal beauty. For to be one with the African woman is a give and take, ying and yang, white and black, a balance between the two that when both parties connect becomes the most glorious example of a union between God's creatures; two opposites, who, rather than combat one another become the other's strength. For the black woman is the white man's strength and he hers, yet this pair, one too young and foolish to understand while the other blinded by his own power and hatred, were destined to falter, for the tikoloshe stood watching as wind howled and rain lashed the farmhouse, the evil spirit grinned for it would have its due.

As our eagle's blush talons gripped, drawing Soepenberg's authority into her frame, so the tikoloshe waited patiently ... for its turn in drawing the spirit from these beings would come.

The eagle reached the height of pleasure, her wings shook in frenzied seizure, at that same moment the rat evacuated his authoritative remainder within our San slave. Soepenberg's dominance was dragged kicking and screaming as a man to the gallows, his time had come and after being measured by Mbaba Mwana Waresa, the Zulu goddess of fertility and rain, he was found wanting.

This was the moment that Soepenberg's transformation from authoritative Boer to Afrikaner scoundrel became complete, his strength absorbed by the black woman during a night of unbridled passion, first Hannah's passing, then the death of a Xhosa youth and finally the coming together of San and Boer.

He stole life from a Xhosa while she wrestled authority from Boer during which the tikoloshe stood by, licking its lips, hidden by the darkness of Africa ... sniffing their souls.

Chapter Twelve: British Intervention

Helios, guardian of oaths and god of sight, sliced cool African savannah with blazing chariot, permitting mortal men analysis of night time activities upon incorruptible dawn. Allowing scrutiny of obscene nocturnal actions, so judgement may be cast, for judgement did silently approached this blonde Boer's tobacco farm yet those populating his household, within and without, slept soundly, serenaded by Africa's rain goddess playing a beautiful ballad of revitalisation upon hut roofs.

The first item of evidence to be witnessed by Soepenberg's swollen eye was a svelte slave's silky skin. His mind entered a state of shock, the white farmer required many minutes to absorb previous nighttide events, a Xhosa slave, armed combat, Arnou saving his bacon, then, hours later in his bedchamber his senses overcome by the scent of sexuality, a potion of promiscuity ... the language of love became a universal translator with which this black woman and white man communicated.

Violence, love ... or was it merely passion expressed sexually? Whichever it may be, the rat experienced revulsion, for he'd sullied himself with the body of an African slave.

She was beautiful, intelligent, skilled in linguistics, for she comprehended the ways of the white man and his needs, she would be the perfect partner if not for her ethnic roots or as people would point out today, his own prejudice.

Men who'd travelled from Holland to the southern Cape of Africa, settling in the Cape Town area had often taken women of the Khoi-San tribe as partners.

Fornication with the African woman a commonplace occurrence, mixed race children its product. Relationships a rare development of said unions, marriage to a native considered beneath a white man's, or at least a Dutchman's station.

The British weren't so prejudice toward their neighbours ... soon to be their colonial burden.

Despite her beauty, smooth skin, fine figure, toned muscle and proud facial features, Soepenberg could not bring himself to call her his, not in any capacity other than master to slave.

A sad state of affairs which even in the 21st century many fail to surmount, for tribalism is human nature and if one does differentiate from the tribe they are to be excluded, even if that deviance be as little as skin tone or architecture of one's nose, it is enough to bring the tribe together against you.

These deep rooted emotions, planted in a man's genetics millions of years ago, which were no doubt of great assistance to he and his tribe's survival and without which the human race would be extinct, today serve against mankind, for in the 21st century man doth possess such weaponry that with the press of a button he might obliterate his enemy ... and himself.

Perhaps having overcome the larger part of prejudice he might listen to his creators, the ancestors, Our Lord and Saviour Jesus Christ, and work out some method by which he may lay down his tools of self-destruction while turning his mind to self-improvement.

However, we are in the 19th century, where man had yet to learn self-destruction on a worldwide scale. For in this day and age, self-improvement made headway, gaining on suicidal tendencies to the point of overtaking them, eras such as these are marked in history as golden ages. So the Dutch had come to the end of theirs while the British overtook.

Soepenberg observed the black beauty lying in his bed, he and Arnou were disturbed by slaves who the rat assigned responsibility of awakening others, getting them fed and to the fields.

A voice boomed causing all to rise and peer from doorways and windows into the courtyard.

"THE BRITISH ARE COMING! THE BRITISH ARE COMING!" shouted a fellow as he beat a tin pot with ladle.

The white rat and black eagle sat up, his ears pricked, her crescent eyes sharpened. Our lovers peered at one another, Arnou smiled yet Soepenberg reciprocated a concerned visage, for this was not the first time British jurisdiction had muscled in on his territory.

Leaping out of bed the rat threw on clothes he'd cast aside the previous evening. Soepenberg buttoned his pants, and as he buttoned yellowed shirt he snapped at our San slave, "Get to work, before they see you've gone!"

Our eagle was taken aback by her lover's insulting tone. She remained in bed, silent and naked, her fine frame reflecting the first rays of Helios peeping through umbrella trees.

Soepenberg gathered her skirt and top, lobbed them into her lap and spat, "Get dressed and get to work, before you join that Xhosa."

Arnou's expression morphed from one of love and joy to cold scorn, a visage only feminine fury is capable of creating; a visage all experienced men fear, for it does signal hard times ahead. Just as African moon is a sure predictor of inclement weather, for should said moon display a circle around its edge, the farmer, sailor or military commander comprehends harsh conditions following Mother Nature's warning.

Equally, if an African woman's visage displays a glowing scowl, the African man and even white man for that matter are headed for rough seas and ought baton down hatches.

Soepenberg was unconcerned with these facts of life for another force of nature had tracked him east to Griqualand, the British Army. Having cast his kind from the Cape Colony then the Orange Free State, they were now present in Griqualand East. These British bastards were something like an ancient curse hunting Soepenberg wherever he settled.

Matters far more pressing were at hand than a San slave's scowl, Soepenberg feared for his property, the British had decided to move in on Griqualand just as Adam Kok III and his council predicted.

The rat dashed from its nest and into morning's rays. His rodent like eyes squinted in sunlight, forcing the Boer to place a bruised hand above troubled brow.

The image which offered itself was one of horror for this was not a small detachment but an entire regiment; it was the King's 60th Royal Rifles, headed by Major General Chelmsford himself.

The King's 60th was founded more than 100 years ago on a different continent.

During 1754 war broke out in North America between British and French. A new method of fighting was required, men armed with rifles fought in a forested American frontier, using dense woodlands as camouflage. Initially given the number 62, they were re-designated as the 60th Royal American Regiment of Foot in 1757.

Their earliest actions being against the French and their allies in the seven year war (1756-1763). Then they engaged the native settlers during Pontiac's rebellion (1763-1766).

The King's Royal Rifles fought in the American War of Independence, the Napoleonic Wars, present at the battle of Waterloo.

During the Victorian era they were engaged in the Indian Mutiny of (1857-1858) where they first encountered their present commanding officer, Major General Chelmsford, a young lad at the time, bearing but an individual one inch row of lace upon the top of his collar with a single crown and a bath star, the mark of a captain, a rank hard won in the Crimean War.

In India he met his friend, then Governor of Bombay, now High Commissioner of South Africa, Henry Bartle, where Frederic serves today, in Africa, as his Adjunct-General.

The hardest man in the British Army backed by its hardest soldiers, men recruited from drinking taverns across England; where a man signed his life to the crown for a shilling a month. Service in the British Army was at the very least a 21 year stretch.

Unlike today, a man may not quit when the going gets tough, it was life or 21 years, or life with a glimmer of hope at the end of the tunnel.

Living conditions did cause many of Her Majesty's Prisons to seem a favourable prospect, for barracks were often overcrowded, added to that they suffered poor sanitation, men were squeezed together as sardines in a tin.

Punishment, again, harsher than common law justice. The death penalty often doled out for mutiny or as little as striking an officer. The lash put to work for many crimes, though a maximum having been set to a mere 50 strokes.

Though excessive in the minds of civilized men of both Africa and Europe, it was nothing compared to the previous century's 2,000 strokes, a death sentence in all but name, for no man was able to survive a flogging of that magnitude.

A small portion of men were permitted to marry, with still fewer allowed to bring their wives overseas. With but a single sheet to obscure man and wife from wandering eyes of foul, sex starved soldiers squashed into barracks at night ... it was far from ideal.

Under those conditions a man does open his mind to the most alien femininity inhabiting far off lands, be it India or Africa.

The men of the 60th King's Royal Rifle Corps were the hardest bastards in Africa, hard living, hard fighting, blessed with little to no love to ease their miserable plight with but a shilling a week and an extra six pence for stoppages (food and sundries), if fortunate.

So, when Soepenberg witnessed these men approach in force, you understand why even a godless low life such as he sensed the fear of Our Lord Jesus Christ shake his frame, liquefying his spine, reducing it to a column of hot wax sliding down his body toward muddy earth.

The British were coming just as they did in the Cape Colony, moving onto the Orange Free State, and now Griqualand East. Wherever slavery was present the meanest bastards on the go did march in unison, tea stained pith helmets bobbing up and down, woollen jackets dyed scarlet red, black trousers with a single red stripe from hip to black leather boot. A thick white strap from shoulder to hip held a small white bag for ammunition and sundries.

By the side of this red snake trotted two men on horseback. The first being Major Chelmsford himself, he distinguished himself even to the layman's eye for his pith helmet, tall as the Drakensberg Amphitheatre in KwaNatal and white as the fabulous cliffs of Dover extricated Chelmsford from every other man in this caravan of calamity. He was an officer and officers didn't stain their helmets. He also bore a cavalry sabre on his left side while a revolver rested on his right.

The man behind, Lieutenant-Colonel Evelyn Wood, rode a chestnut mare, his pith helmet stained with tea, just as his men, setting him apart from other officers serving Queen Victoria on the African Cape.

This was the worst outcome in Soepenberg's mind, for had a herd of elephant, a crash of rhino or even a bloat of hippo appeared moving full steam toward his vulnerable estate, there is something he might have done. Perhaps gathering a group on horseback with rifles and diverting their stampede or at least lessen its blow by bringing down as many creatures as possible. Even without a big game rifle the noise of a well-placed shot would be enough to discourage a rhino from continuing toward his crops and ruining his harvest.

Besides, he could always assess their damage afterwards and make necessary repairs. Yet this British bloat of scarlet snakes, headed by a white lion, would inflict damage upon his business not obvious to the human eye. For these were men of righteousness, defenders of dignity whose knees bent only in the presence of God and Queen Victoria. Colonial warmongers marching forth into foreign lands inspired by the word of God, rounding up slaves owned by decent hard working men ... Boers and black alike ... then setting them free.

Forcing out farmers as British took Boer sovereignty captive, and there was no-one to stop them, for the reach of Russia was inadequate.

The French, bogged down in North and West Africa, were preparing to meet their own colonial subjects on the battlefield. After a defeat in the Franco Prussian war France's African colonies were restless and soon to explode in violence, one of the oldest human stories, violence in exchange for freedom ... or subjection.

The Americans, exhausted by civil war and with a strict policy of non-intervention in foreign affairs were not going to save them, no, it would be up to African tribes to put a halt to the never ending advance of scarlet coated colonists from a tiny isle on the other side of the planet.

Soepenberg's problems were not nearly so grand. He'd experienced this before, twice. He'd lived in a 'free country' only to have the British march in, confiscating not only sovereignty but slaves along with it.
Major General Chelmsford was extending that British tradition, marching into a weakly defended area which no-one wanted twenty years ago. Unfortunately it stood along the path to KwaNatal and the eastern coast.
Perhaps Sarah's attempted kidnapping had triggered this march on Kokstad? Or had this action previously been devised? The failed assault on Bartle's niece providing final justification to shunt the wheels of British power into action, a process rarely reversed.
Either way, it was superfluous to the rat has he observed a white lion sitting proud on a black stallion, trotting toward his property.
The viper's head entered Soepenberg's kraal and halted. Chelmsford and Wood dismounted their steeds, splashing mud in all directions from lacquer boots. The Colour Sergeant blasted orders through a moustachioed mouth, "TO THE RIGHT, SALUTE!"
Each man in the column turned his head ninety degrees to the right and saluted both officers as they walked with typical British confidence alongside the column.

Chelmsford, tall and overbearing, scrutinized each and every soldier. Frederic's mutton chops met upon his top lip projecting a stern and fearsome persona, for this man was a strict disciplinarian, his manner being that of a violent tyrant held at bay via the reins of decorum, a set of leather straps preventing each and every British officer's sensibilities from courting barbarity.

"At ease gentlemen," replied our Victorian General emphasising a grand feline grumble. For a beast, when content, doth seem harmless yet the slightest provocation ends in bloody ill temper, something every man was aware of, that is, every man adorned in scarlet.

Chelmsford redirected his vision from soldiers to courtyard, immediately he was drawn to a Xhosa corpse.

A linen sheet soaked and split by last night's rain presented dark contents much like the seed of the star chestnut tree. A dark kernel hidden within carpel shaped boat.

Chelmsford's boots sloshed to a halt in thick mud, he viewed a battered cadaver while drawing morning air. Fresh dew mixed with a stench of death as small flies buzzed above a young man's remains.

The stern lion's gaze shifted from dead slave to whipping post, only six feet away. Despite heavy rains, sodden earth surrounding a tobacco rack displayed a deep ruddy hue, so deep had one dug a grave for this poor fellow a man might still reckon something dark previously occurred on this patch.

The British General's attitude remained at rest, for as a lad he'd witnessed the horrors of Crimea. A single corpse was insufficient trauma to compel this beast to forsake the stoic shade of his cave, bloodied whipping post a common fixture to the duty of the day ... in the Crimea. Today his duty found him in peaceful lands, soon to become a protectorate of the British Empire, yet death and blood remained a constant component in Chelmsford's life, a rivet on a warship that whether in dry dock during peacetime or the high seas during conflict its presence remained, pinning his life to a vessel of death, holding his existence to Charon's boat as deceased are ferried from the banks of the river Styx to Hades kingdom. Chelmsford's sensibility had been moulded by frequent bloodbaths on the Russian peninsula, so much so he merely scanned the corpse before observing Soepenberg march from his porch.

The Boer was furious, for the British were trespassing on HIS property, an intolerable state of affairs to be sure. To the blonde rat he felt singled out against all others, victimized by Chelmsford and High Commissioner Bartle. A foolish concept, to believe that he were so important as to divert a military column of thousands of men sent to secure the province of Griqualand East, yet both man and woman view the world via their own lens, unable to pull themselves away from its focus before snatching but a peep through the eyeglass of other actors in God's play. "What're you bastards doing here?" shouted the mouse, furious at foreign intrusion upon his kraal.

Lieutenant-Colonel Wood's eyes opened wide as two whirlpools appearing before the bow of a sailing ship … unless navigated properly they'd be sure to draw you into the depths of Poseidon's kingdom yet this Dutch sailor pressed further with his verbal assault, "You," he pointed at Chelmsford with a vulgarity rarely witnessed by those who constituted high society on the Cape of Africa.

The white rat caught not only the lion's concentration but also the full force of his indignation; the beast's head did poke from its cave.

Colour Sergeant Bourne understood this British beast had been disturbed by a Dutch rat and the Devil did quick march six steps behind.

"Yeh YOU," snapped the Boer as our British officer silently removed his brown leather riding gloves, clutching them in a single hand.

"What the bloody hell are you and your bastards doing on my property?" shouted the Boer while trudging through mud filled courtyard.

As rat approached British lion, Soepenberg's mind considered in apprehension, "why were all of these people so quiet?" for not a sound was forthcoming from more than a thousand scarlet soldiers.

The fact of the matter was that no man dared speak before the General, for they understood, beneath a calm upper class surface wrapped in the uniform of Queen Victoria's Royal Army, campaign ribbon's on display, beneath that placid lake lurked a shark.

Upon reaching both officers and halting before Chelmsford, anger ground hard upon Soepenberg's face as a gnarly bull ... yet the moment he stopped, planting his feet, Chelmsford chased fury from Soepenberg's visage with a mighty slap of his leather gloves.

"Control yourself sir!" boomed the British lion as onlookers stood in shock.

Rather than cool the rat's blood, Chelmsford's action served only to antagonize Boer vehemence. Humiliation before his own slaves was more than this vermin was prepared to suffer. Having endured yesterday's beating from a Xhosa slave Soepenberg was abused on his own property once again.

Arnou peered from within the kraal, in her mind she observed two lions wrestling for dominance on the plains of Africa.

A pair of white men locked in combat for the prize of a single woman. Every human being's attention captured by an epic struggle, that is, until the San slave heard a familiar whisper grace her ear, "Do not mistake rat for lion young one."

She spun around, unnoticed by others for they were mesmerised by events unfolding outside.

Stood before Arnou, in the shadows of the main house, it was within touching distance yet our eagle dared not reach out and confirm whether this be apparition or flesh and bone, for Arnou feared what might become of her soul should she mount an investigation.

"What do you want?" squawked the eagle, an attempt to demonstrate bravery which fell somewhat flat.

The old witch grinned, "Cool yourself little eagle, for your time approaches."

"Time, what time?" barked the ebony enchantress.

"Arnou, hold your tongue," snapped Aunty from outside the house.

The eagle turned her head to look at Aunty then back again yet the old crone had vanished once more.

"Who are you talking to?" spoke Aunty as two white men, rooted in damp dirt, faced off beneath Helios' rays.

"No one, no one at all," stated our eagle settling her vision back upon the ruckus.

Chapter Thirteen: The Cat

A ruddy cheeked blonde beast presided over his kingdom, opposed by a tall lion from a misty isle famed for its production of great men, a small piece of land off the coast of Europe still to have its finest hour.

The rat peered upwards, its fury unabated, yet forceful action hovered beyond his grasp for these Englishmen ranked high in the service of honour, decency and all expected of civilized man on a continent filled with dark savagery, and so this Afrikaner's ill temperament was staved, yet the blonde Boer refused to back away.

Soepenberg might easily slip into the night when conducting an abominable agenda, far from those familiar to his visage; but today he remained rooted to his own estate, back against the wall, the light of truth and justice blearing into his eyes, today he must obey this British behemoth or contest its authority, for should he not then Soepenberg's license to dominate this region would fall into question.

"Get off my land, you filthy scum!" barked a rat toward the lion's hardy exterior.

The Englishman's heart enlarged, broadening his men for they understood Soepenberg's attitude would not end in the Dutchman's favour.

Unperturbed, a sneer penetrated the lion's beard as he folded leather riding gloves, surprisingly Chelmsford made no reply.

Soepenberg yelped again, "You people, marching around wherever decent men try to make a living, talking about honour and such, bah! You'd make a stuffed bird laugh! You're all in it for what you can steal, just like these blackies, It's men like me who make something of this land."

To be clear, the phrase "To make a stuffed bird laugh" in plain english would mean "To make a preposterous statement".

"Sir, halt your indignation for but a moment and I shall be on my way," replied the lion having regained his poise after striking the farmer, for he came as a supplicant to this kraal.

"Bugger off back to where you came from and leave me be!" snapped the rat.

"Sir! Restrain your anger, I wish to water my horses, after which I shall bequeath my presence to Kokstad," growled the lion.

The voortrekking vermin sneered into Chelmsford's visage, granting his reach passport to outstrip its grasp, Soepenberg let go another verbal assault, "You and your bastards can fuck off my land ... and go back to that fat pig Victoria while you're at it!"

That was the final straw, the lion roared, drowning out logic and reason while superseding all creatures inhabiting the African savannah, "Colonel!"

Lieutenant-Colonel Evelyn Wood, waiting by Chelmsford's side, replied in short order permitting not half a second to pass, for it seemed to each and every African beast, from elephant to ant, that even Helios did pause his journey in observation of this fateful fracas.

"Yes sir!" replied Wood.

"Give this man four and twenty."

"Sir?"

"I said four and twenty Colonel, now execute my orders."

"Yes sir," Wood turned his head to the front of the column, "Colour Sergeant Bourne!"

A man bearing splendid moustache, tea stained pith helmet with ribbons proudly adorning his chest stepped forward, "Yes sir!"

"You heard the General, four and twenty ..."

Before Wood might finish his sentence Major General Chelmsford interjected, "Don't spare the cat Bourne."

"Understood sir!" replied the moustachioed Sergeant.

"A man is well advised to select but a single struggle, whether he be a dullard or a scoundrel, yet this fool has decided to tackle multiple in his lifetime. Your task is to lash a single struggle from his foul frame, is that understood?" boomed our British lion causing weakness to infect everyday men, not least of all Soepenberg, for he was reduced to a helpless observer in this wicked play.

"Understood General," Sergeant Bourne directed three crimson coated soldiers who secured rifles and moved in on the vile rat.

Taking the blonde scoundrel, one on each arm, the third prepared a rope as they dragged the rat, screaming as a baby pulled from the womb, shrieking its first traumatic breaths of life.

Bourne travelled to the baggage train and collected a cat of nine tails. Another unique item the British had introduced into the world, a shortened whip or flail constructed from a piece of thick naval rope.

At one end the rope was unravelled into nine separated plaits, otherwise known as claws, so named for their ability to lacerate skin off a man's back. The other end displayed a loop at its butt and two knots, between which a man would grasp the cat.

"Drummer Morris ..." Stated Sergeant Bourne, for as with tradition a Drummer dealt this dark discipline. A Drummer usually being an orphaned child with but the British Army or workhouse to turn, his arm wouldn't be so detrimental to a grown man's back.

"Bourne," growled the lion.

"Yes sir?"

"You will dispense the lashing."

Bourne raised his brow, as did every man for they understood this would be no ordinary punishment. With a grown man of Sergeant Bourne's stature behind the cat her claws were sure to cut deep, deep enough to kill a man.

"As you wish sir," replied the Sergeant, cat in hand, "At ease Morris."

The white rat struggled in vain for these men were familiar with a man's preparation when rope is to grace back.

In Her Majesty's Armed Forces the cat was frequent punishment for crimes that today would have a man reprimanded and essentially told not to do it again.

Now admittedly, the severity of punishment did vary since the tentacles of Victoria's military spread across the globe and each army corps was split up, especially when on campaign, punishment became a reflection of the officer allotted charge of proceedings.

Having fought hard in the Crimea Chelmsford acclimatised many habits of command. Those in authority were often men of a previous age, an era defined in severity of punishment. For in the eighteenth century the lash was greater in both frequency and severity.

During the 1700's it was not unknown for a man to receive 1,000 lashes; the Royal Navy particularly brutal upon sailors when at sea, for on the waves discipline is required more so than in any other situation. Men are more likely to mutiny against their captain, resulting in the death of officers.

Rather than a drummer the lowest rank upon the ship, a bosun, would deal out punishment. Due to the number of lashes it was usual to see three or four bosuns waiting to take the cat after the first man's arm showed signs of fatigue.

The captain would make certain he had one bosun who was left handed, so as to give a good even crisscross of claws on the beleaguered sailor's back.

Such brutality was often required in the Crimea. Military rebellions frequent due to men starved via bureaucratic incompetence concerning food supplies; British soldiers often ate half rations, down to salt crackers and salt meat, a salt meat that many couldn't eat due to the fact it afflicted said soldiers with horrendous bouts of diarrhoea.

Large shipments of food, when sent as relief, spoiled due to supply officers missing correct paperwork, military pen pushers refused to take responsibility causing hundreds of tonnes of vegetables to rot away.

The British lost more soldiers to starvation, or as parliament put it "supply issues" than enemy guns.

As a junior officer Chelmsford watched on while incompetents bogged down in bureaucracy forced men to freeze in the midst of famine, soldiers rebelled rather than die of hunger in Russian Winter.

The lash became a frequent companion, death and brutality abound.

Comparatively, in Chelmsford's perception, the lash of today was rather sparse and of reduced intensity. Our General often witnessed men receive fifty lashes for drunkenness while on duty, for desertion one to three hundred depending on the officer they stood before.

If a boy were found guilty of any crime meriting the lash he often received a separate cat.

The boy's cat, or better known as "the boy's pussy", possessed but five tails of smooth fibre. Yet if convicted by court martial, he would often suffer the adult cat for crimes such as mutiny.

Sergeant Bourne approached his Afrikaner objective, a foul man wearing leather trousers and yellow cotton shirt. The blonde Boer's back braced before Bourne while his face peered toward British officers, Major General Chelmsford in particular.

Having secured the rat, three soldiers moved away and stood beside one another.

"At your convenience Mr Bourne," stated the lion, inaugurating a tethered Afrikaner's journey to Hell and back.

Bourne tore away a dirty shirt, raised his whip hand and for a moment its tails obscured the light of Helios rising over African savannah, then it rendezvoused with soft flesh.

A mighty crack filled atmosphere bringing all who watched on, slaves, soldiers, military magistrate and spectres hiding amongst shadows, to a silence.

Soepenberg stopped struggling, resisting the urge to demonstrate distress his vision fixed upon his mortal enemy, the British bastard who'd hounded his people out of their homes twice before.

"ONE!" shouted Colonel Evelyn Wood.

Bourne raised his arm again as thick blood travelled a canyon forged but moments before upon the aft of a beleaguered Boer.

Again, Bourne thrust his arm down, *CRACK*, again the terrible noise of rope stick beating the drum of a man's back rang out over African fields.

The slaves, Xhosa, Malay and San gained no satisfaction for they did suffer more than a man's lot in life and to witness this English extravagance shook their bones ... all but Arnou, for she'd been scorned and in the heat of an emotional furnace forgot her position in life, in her mind he did suffer proper correction after slighting this morning's advances.

"TWO," shouted Wood.

Soepenberg's expression didn't change while hot blood coursed stern quarters, flowing as spring rains traveling the Buffalo River.

Chelmsford found Soepenberg's demeanour somewhat disturbing, for his back displayed no previous evidence of the cat's claws.

Bourne raised his arm again, obscuring red sky *CRACK*.

"THREE," called Wood.

"Halt," stated Chelmsford, "again Bourne."

Bourne nodded, "Yes sir," raising his arm Bourne injected further brawn into barbarity and lashed the Afrikaner's back with all his might, cutting deeper into flesh *CRACK*.

"THREE," stated Wood in a somewhat inquisitive tone.

Chelmsford nodded into Bourne's eyes and the Colour Sergeant continued to strip white flesh from its owners back, yet during the entire process Soepenberg refused to cower beneath the shade of British cat as claws tore skin, slashing deep, scarring both body and psyche.

After two dozen strikes and in case you're wondering, that's two dozen proper strikes, for if one were deemed too tame the lion did not add it to the toll and so the true tally was closer to thirty.

By this time the rat was exhausted, semi-conscious he lay in earth muddied by streams of blood, blackening the ground as had his Xhosa slave, their pain and misery indistinguishable. Yet the Blonde Boer would not have given one of his slaves four and twenty, for that man would be unable to work the next day. The lash was intended to deter bad behaviour not inflict long term or permanent disability, possibly death.

The whip was employed, at most, to leave a psychological wound yet Chelmsford was not so impeded.

Out here in Colonial Africa discipline was a requirement, should one man start acting the fool punishment must be swift and merciless.

Chelmsford had watched grown men whipped to death in the Crimea for the crime of stealing from locals, rather than starve on Queen Victoria's meagre rations.

If provisions were paltry on the Crimean peninsula then mercy was but a fable, a myth passed around night time campfires while both man and beast froze to death.

Upon returning to merry old England the majority allowed their attitude to remain on that peninsula ... Chelmsford was not amongst them.

The Crimea existed in him as much as the day he charged a Russian artillery battery under the command of the Earl of Cardigan. A military action immortalised six weeks later in Tennyson's poem "The Charge of the Light Brigade".

Chelmsford was a ruthless commander who followed orders no matter how insane they might seem to you or I. Some men would call him a fool for doing so, others courageous.

One such edict handed down to the High Commissioner for Southern Africa was the elimination of slavery; a practice Chelmsford found particularly disagreeable, for he was a Christian, his faith discovered at the Battle of Balaclava during that fateful charge.

And so, when the edict of his Queen, the Queen of Africa, did mesh with the Major General's faith our white lion arose, walking out of his cave, erect at its entrance, releasing a mighty roar heard across the plains of Africa, causing hyena, wild dogs and vultures to quiver in fear that this righteous beast with the hand of Queen Victoria on one shoulder and that of Our Lord and Saviour Jesus Christ the other, may fall upon their vile stinking nests. Today the white lion did stumble upon one such den of inequity, and he was having none of it.

The slave owner was whipped to the point he could no longer stand. Once untied Soepenberg slumped onto muddy ground, some felt pity, others watched in horror, Chelmsford glared quietly upon a foul demon who'd enslaved his fellow man, coining human misery into gold ... Soepenberg had discovered why the love of money is the root of all evil.

"Wood, these slaves are free by order of the High Commissioner," stated the lion inserting hands inside leather gloves.

"Yes sir," replied Wood.

Lieutenant-Colonel Wood took a group of men and went hut to hut.

"Bourne, see to it the animals are watered," stated Chelmsford.

Bourne returned the cat to its red bag, "Yes sir, what about him sir?" he gestured toward Soepenberg, now lain flat on tainted ground, passing in and out of consciousness.

"Those who plough evil and those who sow trouble do reap it."

"Sir?"

"Job chapter 4 verse 8."

"Oh, I see sir …" Sergeant Bourne remained somewhat bemused.

"Let him remain Sergeant, if the Lord doth wish he live he will make it so."

"Yes sir," Bourne nodded at three redcoats waiting to peel Soepenberg off the ground. Instead of doing so they moved back into formation while Bourne organised troops.

As the reality of freedom descended upon the kraal murmurs transformed into rumbles much like a herd of approaching elephant; newfound liberty unfolded as a sweet orchid opening to the sun and so enlightenment of opportunity aroused native senses, a symphony of independence cracked once suffocating atmosphere. Rather than drums of oppression, the horn of victory released a melody of freedom over this tiny patch of Africa.

Tribal thoughts having no sooner grasped their unburdening did quickly turn to evil, for many men took to looting the estate while its owner died at the base of his own whipping post.

Some were satisfied to accost whatever unchained hands might grasp in the form of provisions before accompanying the British to Kokstad. From there they might find legitimate work or return to their families in KwaNatal.

Many Malay and San decided to work until they could afford the journey back to Cape Town. Some headed to Port Elizabeth and other cities established by the British in the Cape Colony.

Arnou stepped over her former master, her tall figure blocking the eye of Helios beating down upon semi-conscious rat.

She was a woman scorned, a woman who'd opened herself, a spread eagle who'd granted this creature the privilege of probing her vulnerabilities. In return she expected this white man to raise her status from black slave to San Queen. Instead, rejection was Arnou's only reward.

Men are rejected by women throughout their lives, its occurrence not so heart wrenching once frequency overtakes hindrance, eventually such an event becomes natural course when travelling the river that is manhood. Yet a woman is not nearly as experienced in this area and when set upon the rapids of rejection she doth find herself adrift in its furious flow, unable to control her actions, both mind and body respond on impulse and so she becomes a slave to passion, pride and a woman's rage.

The eagle circled above the rat as its muddied visage glanced upwards observing a sharp black beak and stinging crescent eyes. The African eagle sneered and spat onto his face, Xhosa men watch from the side lines, some smiled in satisfaction, others nodded heads in approval. Arnou lobbed harsh words at the rat, just as an eagle will drop rocks from a great height to break open an egg, "Now I am the ruler and you the captive."

He lifted his hand, moving but six inches above foul dirt for the cat had sapped his strength and soon his soul. The eagle's sneer widened, transmitting a brand of smug satisfaction only a woman might gain from observing her former lover in his death throes, "Save your might for the Devil, for he will judge you and your rotten deeds you filthy piece of white shit!"

She spat a second time, her actions drained hope from the Boer's heart; this further loss of fortitude caused his arm to flop back into dirt while his face splashed rusty earth.

Soepenberg sensed hooves of a demonic beast beating ground, coming to collect his soul, their cadence as clear as Zulu war drum.

Aunty took Arnou by her shoulders, "Come child, we must leave this place. The longer we remain the sooner evil will befall us."

By sundown the farm was vacant but for a man and his dying breaths. All alone beneath a whipping post he'd erected, property looted, his former home laid bare to Mother Nature's menace just as the white rat's spirit was exposed to Lucifer's delight.

For a few minutes Soepenberg lay dead, his soul no longer tethered to its mortal frame, journeying the ether, cast out by God in retribution for his sin, sent to the fiery pit ruled by the Prince of Lies, where he'd suffer torment for eternity.

Then ... out of dusk's gloom a figure trod lightly upon earth, crouching down an old crone breathed life back into the white man's corpse.

The smoke of his spirit blasted back into his feeble frame and with a loud cough then a splutter Soepenberg rebounded into reality.

The African witch, an old woman's corpse possessed by a sorcerer, made living quarters for another tikoloshe ... for that is what Soepenberg had become, an evil man when alive, now dead, the living dead, he became tikoloshe, an evil spirit drawn from the nether world by demonic request with the permission of the Devil himself. Soepenberg was returned to the land of the living with but a single purpose ... revenge.

His wounds healed and vitality returned until the Afrikaner arose from muddy pit to enter his home. On discovering vandalism inflicted by former slaves Soepenberg became angered, for within this man or demon or both, only negative emotions did exist.

Discarding clothes he removed a floorboard in his bedroom and from underneath picked a large purse filled with gold coin.

He grinned, the blonde Boer was to return to Kokstad and wreak havoc upon those who'd slighted him ... one person in particular did fill his thoughts, for the image of her spitting from high was seared into his brain by African sun.

Soepenberg, not the man, but the demon, his dead spirit summoned by African sorcery, a tikoloshe inside a man's body would reap revenge.

Chapter Fourteen: Kokstad's Fall

Residents of Kokstad observed a dust cloud, some wondered if a herd of elephant approached to drink from the Mzimhlava River; a long winding stretch of water originating at what is now the Lesotho border, meandering at a leisurely pace before pouring into the Indian Ocean.

Adam Kok III had a better understanding, his old eyes able to divine truth from a haze threatening his namesake. A wave of crimson did peep above the horizon, a foreboding crest crashing upon his small municipality.

"What is this I witness?" stated Doctor Albronda squinting into the distance, "a crimson flood from Mount Currie? I thought it too late in the year."

Adam did not answer but Reverend Dower, flanking Adam's other side, did speak on the matter, "Have no fear Doctor, for God will never forget the needy."

Adam, his vision secured to an ever growing red boundary, spoke in a downcast tone, "Reverend, I fear Griqualand East shall not survive this christening."

"I am made aware General Chelmsford is a strict man of the faith, or am I to be mistaken?" replied the clergyman.

"Aye, that he is Reverend yet the Devil doth reside in his heart, from time to time," sighed the toned legislator charged with securing a nation out here on the Eastern Cape of South Africa.

"We are all sinners, even the most square rigged of fellows," replied the preacher.

Adam nodded his head, "True father, yet I feel our fate has been decided ... it has been done."

The trio watched on as British brinksmanship rapidly approached, their mark further blemishing golden horizon. Terrible fate dawned upon Kokstad as morning sun doth dominate sky.

Distant drums beat as thousands of men descended upon Kokstad. The city abandoned all production and commerce to observe a crimson coated army of condemnation enter its city limits, reaching a halt before their leaders ... General Chelmsford and Colonel Wood dismounted.

Approaching a bemused trio, bemused save Adam Kok III for he understood what was to occur. His raiding party into Cape Town, hunting but a single swan, had failed.

Griqua huntsmen no doubt squawked to authorities providing Bartle with an excuse to deploy his brother in incorruptible deeds Kokstad way.

With barely enough men and arms to fight off cattle raiders, who often made forays into this land, the Griqua people had no means by which to resist British incursion. Compromise became the order of the day, or more to the point, faith in God that the Almighty would bestow mercy upon the Griqua people after so many previous hardships.

Chelmsford sheathed a horsewhip in its saddle and approached the threesome.

Adam mimicked a powerful warthog, black with thick broad shoulders flanked by grey horse and white ox, an aged trio grizzled by mortal misery. For they, like the lion, are chieftain to God's smaller creatures who follow a path cleared by their leader's titanic strains, and when a lion or warthog's life is cut short by almost supernatural persistence another great beast, previously unknown, doth rise to the challenge and foray forward, slicing through severity, breaching unyielding barricades which contrive human life, so slighter creatures may walk a less bothersome route.

So the Kokstad Warthog and Chelmsford Lion did face one another as insignificant mortals cowered on the periphery.

"Adam Kok III I presume?" inquired Chelmsford, for they'd yet to meet in person.

"General Chelmsford?" replied this black warthog, the warthog a symbol of African vigilance, its dry skin sagging in dispassionate dawn air, hand extended.

The people of Kokstad held a collective breath while waiting on the lion's response, for this would set the tone of their fate.

It was so quiet birds could be heard chirping to one another on Kokstad's outskirts, such silence prevailed that insects rubbing wings might be tracked. A seminal moment in the history of South Africa, reason being that Victorian history does influence modern day; for what took place this day will have repercussions upon an entire people centuries into the future, something Adam Kok III might have foreseen yet Chelmsford remained either unaware or unconcerned.

The lion removed his leather riding gloves and shook the hog's hand, "It's a pleasure to meet you sir."

The crowd exhaled, eyes glued to opposing parties.

"May I ask why you've visited our fair city?" inquired Adam.

"I believe you are quite aware as to my purpose in Kokstad, sir."

"I'm afraid I ..."

The lion raised his voice, it went from deep purr to low growl, enough so lesser beasts became nervous, "Sir, I must warn you, I do not endure inauthenticity at any time of day, least of all morning."

Adam Kok III cleared his throat, yet before readdressing the General, Reverend Dower intervened, "General, may I speak on Adam's behalf?"

"Please proceed Reverend."

"Dower, Reverend Dower."

"Do continue Reverend Dower."

"Kokstad is a simple God fearing conurbation of pious men and women, the sight of your army marching within its limits has left my flock somewhat overwhelmed. Pray, in the name of the Lord, would you elude your purpose in travelling here, or would thou accuse a servant of God to walk the path of the Devil?"

Upon such an accusation the lion lost his growl, for he respected all servants of God, considering himself a man who's ultimate goal lay in in the Lord's rationale, "Certainly not Reverend ... I will say it has come to light, through the mechanism of Cape Town courts, that a dastardly plot to kidnap the high commissioner's daughter did originate in Kokstad, specifically that building," Chelmsford gestured toward the Town Hall where leaders held council and the decision had been made, a decision which set this chain of events into motion, tempting a scarlet snake of colonial domination within Kokstad's limits, hissing about a dark skinned warthog.

Despite an advantage of home territory and superior numbers marshalled by this sounder of black beasts, the British lion did outweigh him in power, precision and persistence. And so Adam was reduced to his base elements, as an alchemist scrambling night and day to discover the hidden method of creating gold, motivated by avarice and driven mad by sin, for the greatest sin is the love of money.

Yet Adam was driven by virtues, freedom and love of his people, the Griquas. With this in his heart he did search tirelessly for an answer to his tribulations. Distilling strength and percolating power through the soil of persistence, hoping to catch those elements that are best in man, in order he grow the Griqua people as strong as the Xhosa or perhaps, God willing, as resolute as the Zulu.

Yet despite his machinations Adam Kok III was left with a discombobulated band, more interested in personal pleasure than cultivating a community which might stand the test of time; a community unable to hold fair beside Xhosa to the East, Zulu to the North and British to the West.

To Adam's disappointment, while surrounded by the leading nations of Africa and predominant people of Europe, it was not to be, for these nations were fixed to clash with one another and when trapped between hippo of Africa and woolly mammoths of Europe, even the rhino doth quiver, for not only does he sense terror in his bones as the charge begins but the very ground beneath his feet doth tremble.

Usually benign beasts, roused to war, cause lesser creatures to reduce in spirit, from the mighty rhino to the lowest rodent.

Adam, reduced by British integrity, relaxed his stance from defiant to defensive, a negligible yet significant difference when in heightened situations such as these. Chelmsford did note Adam's transformation in his mind, for he'd spent his career sizing the enemy before battle and he did perceive a remodel in his opponent's body language as well as attitude.

The Griqua leader reduced in spirit as a priest having righteousness drained by the Pope. The black hog did accept his fate and on receiving the lion's judgement he silently awaited sentence, for what else might he do? Men and women did mutter to one another mimicking a flock of birds chirping in the trees, while rays of Helios warm both field and savannah first thing at dawn.

Chelmsford's hand remained fixed on the Town Hall while clutching brown leather riding gloves, his white pith helmet beamed righteousness while its brass badge reflected virtue. A scarlet tunic with epaulettes, white leather straps crossing his chest supporting cavalry sword and revolver, a pair of jet black trousers with single red line on each leg traveling hip to hem, a pair of mud stained patent leather boots, our British General was truly a daunting sight.

Relaxing his long arm Chelmsford did glare at the black hog, his lack of interjection answer enough for only shame remained, orbiting as a demonic moon around this discredited lawmaker, mocking both night and day and when full moon doth appear, all Griqua living on that heavenly body do witness its stigma, some noting its existence with confusion, others derision, yet all shocked by their lack of foreknowledge.

"Is this true?" asked Reverend Dower of the warthog.

"Aye, it is so," replied the old Griqua to a wave of chirps and gasps.

Initially townsfolk chattered on what he'd done, before their minds turned to what might become of them, for humans are selfish creatures prone to consider themselves before others.

Reverend Dower glanced toward the sky and muttered, "May our Lord and Saviour Jesus Christ show mercy upon us this day."

Chelmsford was touched by the Reverend's plea, for not only was he a man of God but he sensed an affinity with Adam Kok III.

Most men in this world when offered a great opportunity would reject it, for all opportunity involves an element of risk, two ingredients thriving upon one another, mimicking their twin. The greater the risk, then, so in proportion, opportunity does increase.

For this reason men will often reject opportunity and play it safe, for in life the majority's objective is to avoid failure rather than succeed at all costs.

Chelmsford and Adam were not amongst their number, they'd risen in status as men who lived by the maxim "carpe diem" or "seize the day", and saw risk for what it was, the progenitor of success.

Yet today Adam was to suffer the consequences of this philosophy for sometimes in life, man best take the cautious trend and reject triumph, omitting opportunity in order he avert disaster.

As men do change the course of a mighty life giving river, not because they wish their crops to shrivel and die but because that river is often plagued by flood. It is a superior philosophy to manage its course and build a dam, use those lands created for food and raising a family while transporting its soul sustaining flow where needed.

And so, rather than take caution, perhaps because the flood was already upon him, Adam took action without sufficient contemplation. On the advice of Soepenberg, a fellow who lay dead in his own kraal, whipped to death … or so everyone believed. On the rat's foolhardy counsel, Lucifer his advocate, Adam surged forth in an attempt to secure liberty by denying another hers.

The fact of failure was no surprise to Reverend Dower for "Those who plough iniquity and sow trouble will reap the same," – Job 4:8.

"It is under the authority of the High Commissioner for South Africa, Sir Henry Bartle Fere and Her Majesty Queen Victoria, that I accept Griqualand East's status as a protectorate of the British Empire," stated Chelmsford in a matter of fact tone, his visage reflecting an escarpment of rock jutting from Mount Currie, harsh and unyielding no matter the angle of approach.

Doctor Albronda let out a chuckle, for this chain of events seemed preposterous to a man grounded in the world of medicine, "This is ludicrous!" barked the doctor, his protruding belly leaping up and down as words exited its frame.

Colonel Wood attached a stern set of eyes upon the man, as two torches threatening a hyena. And so an apprehensive animal will retract from former enterprise upon witnessing righteous blaze, valour evapourated by British flame.

Doctor Albronda peered left to observe serious expressions, that of Adam and the Reverend. Mount Currie present in countenance, a precipice he surmised no man, even the most able climber, might overcome. Today the leaders of the Griqua nation were to set down climbing gear and surrender to this British edifice before them, lest they risk total ruin.

Adam had rolled the dice in Cape Town and lost. Today he was faced with putting all of his and his people's chips on 13 then letting it ride … or, depositing what remained of his purse in the Bank of England.

Adam decided to play it safe and bank what little his people possessed under an agreement with the British by which he might be assured protection versus Xhosa and Zulu raiding parties.

"Do you see the men behind me sir?" asked Chelmsford of Doctor Albronda.

"I do sir," replied the Doctor, somewhat quizzical as to the nature of his statement.

"This force does contain the most experienced fighting men the British Empire has to offer, conversely and equally," his pitch deepened as if the course of conversation were being lowered to a region unseen by human eye, "many standing behind my person are amongst the most detestable scoundrels and knaves to be drafted from Her Majesty's Prisons.

I pray I am not provoked to loosen their leash and blight the good people of Griqualand East, for these villains desire little besides rape, murder and pillage."

Doctor Albronda drew deeply, uncertain if he were dizzy from the giddy heights of Mount Currie or drowning in the depths of Lake St Lucia, named by a Portuguese navigator on December 13th, 1575, the day of the feast of St Lucy.

Reverend Dower returned fire, for this could proceed no further than a war of words, and if that were to be the case this erudite priest was by far the most suitable fellow to lead the charge, "General Chelmsford, really, that's quite enough."

The British lion withdrew, his eyelids relaxed, claws retracting alongside his tone, for he was a Christian man and so resisted both petty recrimination and obtuse celebration in the same measure, rather, the lion rationed his temperament to produce a man of manners befitting Victoria's uniform.

"Forgive me Reverend," stated our pithed veteran.

Reverend Dower continued, "I understand Adam has permitted Kokstad's crooked to besmirch the reputation of its whole, but in the name of Jesus Christ such foolishness surely does not warrant Cape Town's miscreants despoil the women and children of this municipality?"

"Gentlemen," stated Adam Kok III, "Let us speak in the privacy of my chambers rather than air grievance or make threats which, like a crime, once born witness by public eye cannot be returned and is thus forced to meet resolution."

On this all men did agree, for if tempers were to fray in the public arena of Kokstad's main fairway, promises may have been made in the heat of anger which honour demand be seen to terrible ends.

Behind closed doors, fury which slips the tongue via the Devil's greasing may be retrieved. Decrees disclosed behind official palisades are quickly emancipated from exposure to the critical cataracts of Kokstad.

With less on the line, for an Englishman does hold honour above all else, reconciliation may be forged from the furnace of chaos despite each one of Hell's demons exerting itself on Beelzebub's bellows.

Less than an hour later two British officers, pith helmets resting in their wallah's arms, exited Kokstad's town hall followed by a rather downcast delegation of ministers and Adam Kok III himself.

The people of Kokstad were informed they'd not be going to war for they'd become a part of the British Empire, this was met by lacklustre response.

For a Boer farmer it was an ill omen, despite retaining its own law and jurisdiction Griqualand East's eventual annexation was unavoidable, at which point the forced emancipation of slaves became inevitable.

Griquas were undecided, for the British Empire had always treated them favourably. Some Griquas welcomed the Empire in belief they'd deal with frequent raids from Xhosa and Zulu country. Other Griquas were suspicious not only of the Empire but the white man in general. True to their nature, Griquas were split, part white, part black their identity struggle continued, destined to return to Cape Town. For Griqualand was as doomed as their attempt to strike out, delivering these people nothing but hardship.

As Adam explained the situation to his people, Chelmsford made a noteworthy detour to Strachan&Co's trade store, a short walk from where they stood.

As Colonel Wood addressed the men, Arnou, having travelled with the British baggage train, watched silently from across the street.

She witnessed something odd. It was obvious a meeting of significance took place. For Donald Strachan stood outside his store, Chelmsford halted before him. Although our former San slave could not fathom their words she was aware of a strange chant, similar to a Catholic prayer. Strachan did recite a set of words she failed to make sense of, yet she, a skilled linguist, was familiar with all languages spoken in this region both foreign and domestic.

Chelmsford replied with a corresponding parable in what must have been the same tongue yet she could not be certain.

Nevertheless, both men understood these recantations, perhaps a secret code? For they exchanged knowing looks all the time and sealed their encounter with a devilish handshake. After witnessing their hands meet and twist as snakes turning on one another in combat, a chill touched Arnou's spine.

Our emancipated African was confounded, secret signs, Hellenic hymns and reverent regard merged to form a scene captivating her senses.

As if suspended for a moment in time while others remained occupied at the other end of the fairway, she alone scrutinized a sacred revival of a dark text perhaps bound in a leather tome, hidden deep within the Vatican's walls.

Our black eagle did not miss the mark totally for as she soared above, eves dropping interactions, it became apparent that business occurred between these fellows yet their transaction consisted of neither good nor coin ... but knowledge, the most valuable commodity to a British General in these colonies.

For these two fellows were familiar in so far as they were men of the lodge, that is, they were Freemasons. An organisation shrouded in mystery, its origins unknown yet its rituals have something to do with the master architect Hiram Abiff, a man murdered by three ruffians after they'd failed to obtain the master masons' secrets to King Solomon's Temple.

Lodges existed throughout the British Isles run by Grand Lodges, all independent of one another, yet one mason will recognise another, even in this frontier on the other side of the globe.

For symbols within the tradesman's shop, though meaningless to the uninitiated were clear beacons to a fellow mason. The masonic square and compass within Strachan's store was one such symbol by which allegiance was identified.

Upon making contact in Cape Town, Commissioner Bartle, another Freemason, did request he keep an eye upon the Griqua.

It's no coincidence that when you look back in history so many leaders were members of the lodge, for the Freemasons had become the intelligence network of the British Empire.

A General or Governor, also a member of the lodge, would recognise his fellow mason and use that intelligence to plan the rise of his career and the expansion of the Empire with outcomes favourable toward freemasonry.

And so Chelmsford made contact with his informant in Griqualand East, the man who'd made him aware of the plot against the high commissioner's daughter.

Troop strength and weakness transmitted by coded telegraph or upon visiting Cape Town or Port Elizabeth, where Chelmsford resided on his estate.

An excuse for invasion discovered, abduction averted, plans to march on Griqualand finalised and executed, the white lion approached his brother and spoke in Latin while exchanging hand gestures.

Strachan opened the door to his empty store and the pair walked inside to conduct further business, away from prying eagle.

Arnou, wrapped in mystery, shook her head before making her way to visit a tikoloshe masquerading as a sangoma, for she too had unfinished business in Kokstad.

Chapter Fifteen: Vengeance is Mine

Released from the rat's nest Arnou's struggle had concluded. Her sentence served, sapience informed our salient beauty to flee the evil which inhabited this municipality of malevolence, yet youth and wisdom are two points great in distance on the chart of life.

For in their natural state all substances are of a coarse nature, that is to say unrefined, not having passed through the process of life so far as to shed those properties which prevent it from becoming undisturbed in deep deliberation until a solution betrays itself.

Arnou was a substance of natural beauty traded at great price across the known world. Once copper, zinc and other metals are separated she becomes pure gold, a symbol not only of wealth but wisdom.

Unfortunately Arnou had not removed her imperfections and so when a fork in life's road became apparent, rather than err on the side of caution as a gold sovereign, she instead took the path of impetuous youth, and so thoughts of revenge swirled within her mind obscuring prudent exit.

For youth is quick to act, often to its own detriment, whereas age doth bring contemplative experience and Arnou had nowhere she might seek advice, for all remaining slaves had dispersed, not that she would've listened had even Aunty expressed warning of such foolish inclination, for it is written, "Never take your own revenge, beloved, but leave room for the wrath of God, for it is written, "Vengeance is Mine, I will repay," sayeth the Lord." – Romans 12:19.

Our emancipated San made her way through the Khoi-san quarter of Kokstad's slums. The Xhosa lived close by yet fear of sorcery kept them in check, why, to confront a tikoloshe was pure lunacy, for grown men did baulk at the thought of opposing such ancient evil.

Stepping through the hut's entrance the tikoloshe's voice crackled within a dark nebula of necromancy, "You have returned little eagle."

A set of pure white eyes lit up in the hut's rear, opportunity became stark reality, our black eagle smiled in satisfaction as with one arm she pushed thick curtain aside while the other reached toward her leather belt.

The Sangoma's eyes twitched, divining the hawk's intent, "You come to me dagger in belt and blade in heart."

"I do," stated the African youth as she stepped inside.

Suddenly a chill came over Arnou despite warm African summer without ... for within Siberian winter did smother dank atmosphere.

Bright eyes floated, waist high, in the darkness of frosted tundra flashing with joy as ill emotion befell our former slave.

Arnou halted for a moment, taking her surroundings into account, something truly evil did occupy this place yet her heart and mind did set her body with the task of dispatching this beast to the darkest corner of Hell it'd escaped from.

Taking another step forward Arnou drew dagger from belt, cold African steel glinted across a tikoloshe's visage yet rather than sow seeds of fear inside the old crone's heart it evoked delight, for evil begets evil and there is nothing more sumptuous to the demonic than the malevolent, for it is the currency by which they sustain their wicked existence in the world of the living.

"Ahhh, revenge," crackled the witch as if she were a sailor sighting shore for the first time in many months, witnessing womanly form spread upon a sandy beach, that perfect hourglass shape, his desire bubbling to the brim as a powerful broth marooned on hot stove, he has no other mind than to satisfy his hunger.

"Yes, revenge!" stated our San hawk, crescent eyes lifting with each inflection, frothing at the lip, separating meat from bone in order she may dine on vengeance, a dish the Russians say is best served cold, but here in Africa, when blood boils, the heat of fate doth bring about revenge.

Sangoma and San traded African proverbs with one another, "Only a fool does test the depths of a river with both feet."

Arnou sneered as she took another step, coming closer to red coals on the floor, "If you wish to make a tattoo, blood must be spilt."

At that moment the old witch's mouth opened, displaying crooked teeth resembling a line of forsaken tombstones. The crone cackled, mocking our young lady, intent on murder.

Lowering her voice to meet its crouched frame the old crone whispered, "You have done well child. Your capacity for hatred is substantial, join me and I shall cultivate your contempt, become my apprentice and together we can control the fate of men for generations."

Arnou looked down at the shadowy figure on the opposite side of dying embers; snorting through her nostrils she spat words from her mouth, "Pah! This is the end of your foul residency. I would never turn my hand to evil!"

Again the crone mocked our approaching eagle; the witch seemed to have no concern toward looming fate, "Never? You murdered an innocent on her sick bed or perhaps your recollection is limited by convenience?"

"I was manipulated into committing that heinous act," replied the hawk as its dark complexion glowed by the light of ashen faggots occupying the centre of the sangoma's hut.

At that moment both creatures became visible to one another, our eagle pulsated with malice, the crone cackled in equal measure yet her emotion was one of rapture for it did relish these occasions. For when existence is eternal, pleasures are fewer and farther between, a morsel of malice, a slice of spite and grain of grievance ... barely sufficient to nourish the most ancient evil walking this continent.

"Tricked? You sought I. The eagle has flown into a cloud, a cloud of self-hatred," cackled the crone as smoke rose from embers exiting the hut's roof.

Yet the smoke of passion inside our San's heart and soul had no hope of liberation for despite emancipation she remained a slave, fettered by fury, the morbid shackles of self-hate blocking both mind and vision, all Arnou could see was an old witch, logical thought obscured by fog of revenge. Vengeance intensified with but a single passage from Arnou's frame, a long a blade of steel, its exit a dagger's tip.

Arnou heard the sound of tarpaulin shifting, was it the wind or had another soul entered the hut? Our San slave's sneer widened as the wicked spectre peered over Arnou's shoulder with opaque eyes, "I will not be taken by one of your tricks, not again. Today I call the dance, not you," stated our eagle with utter confidence as her blade glinted in the light of red coals. Emancipated by God ... enslaved by the Devil.

Our eagle lurched in her first attack, diving from a cloud of smoke, exposing herself to all, claws out ... yet rather than lunge forward Arnou felt a pair of hands, one gripped her throat while the other grasped the wrist of her knife hand. Next a familiar voice whispered, "You murdered Hannah?"

She struggled with the dagger as emancipated human reverted to San slave, not by work of man but the Devil, Arnou's bloody minded revenge mutated into misgiving while a stealthy demon employed superior strength, holding her body to his while simultaneously disarming Arnou.

Arnou turned, eyes fastening themselves to the visage of what could not be, she scrutinized its ridges and whirlpools as a cartographer navigating straights where Gorgons had cast their gaze, petrifying sea into the most dangerous rocky water way.

For our black eagle did witness the white rat, returned from the dead, raised from hell by a tikoloshe and in scrutinizing this monstrosity so she had become a slave to evil, just as he.

"Master?" whispered our San slave in a weak tone.

"I'm here," replied an Afrikaner phantasm made flesh, for it had touch, presence, being ... it, he, was real.

"Forgive me Master, I did it for us, so we could be together, I did it for love," the eagle's emotions pulled out of a revenge fuelled dive, swooping up into self-pity and regret as salt water did course her cheeks.

The blonde Boer, a resurrected spirit returned to the land of the living so he may act out HIS master's bidding, for Soepenberg was in debt to the old crone, a debt he was bound to reimburse in blood and gore.

The tikoloshe's face filled with mirth, expanding as an old animal skin carrying sustenance on a woman's back yet this sustenance was spiritual in nature, dark in hue, black as burnt embers, stygian as a queen of the night tulip, bleak as the tikoloshe's heart and grim as its perverse desires.

"Love?" stated the white rat, "Only hatred endures for your kind," he cast the dagger aside and with both hands took Arnou by her throat.

The hellion, once cast into Satan's fiery pit and recalled to Africa by a tikoloshe, was set on vengeance, not merely concerning Arnou but upon an entire race of people. Soepenberg's blue eyes sparkled reflecting both crackling embers and cackling sangoma, her horrific tone filled the air frightening all from the scene of another dastardly murder.

For the first time since his resurrection the rat sensed something … satisfaction did enter his frame. For now he was tikoloshe, void of joy save via another's suffering … and the misery of African's, black Africans providing nourishment superior by far.

As dishes laid out at a banquet, some more satisfying than others yet all originating from a single menu; a hors d'oeuvre of despair, malady soup, agony for appetizers, fish caught off the coast of retribution, malice for main course and depression for dessert.

There was no room in Soepenberg's being for love, pity or empathy … forgiveness was poison to these foul creatures.

Arnou let a strained squawk escape while an evil beast choked her spirit, wrangling it into the nether world … as she died, eyes wide open, staring into his, her spirit unshackled from its flesh frame to be consumed by Soepenberg, for he was required to dine on living souls in order he combat the gravity of evil dragging his spirit into Hell, this was the Devil's tithe, split between Satan and the tikoloshe with but a few crumbs remaining so this Dutch demon might sustain his existence.

Last night Soepenberg peered into Arnou's eyes while making love, taking pleasure in one another's psyche, the emotion of lust mixing with love. Yet today horror and hatred merged, dragging Arnou's soul out of her body to be consumed by the man she once loved and respected. And so another African spirit was devoured, not the first and by no means the last for he who sows the wind shall reap the whirlwind, and so it was.

Arnou's lifeless frame crumpled to the ground, observed by a jubilant geriatric, its cloudy eyes bloomed with rapture, filled by the dark mirror that is death, its backing a thin layer we call oblivion yet this stinking creature, crouched in foulness, relished each passing moment for the purpose of its existence was defined on that terrible backing.

The old witch fixed her strange stare upon Soepenberg, her new apprentice. The white man held an odd expression, as an addict who'd smoked a bowl of opium for the first time in many years, relaxation and tranquillity befell his visage while he kicked back for a moment. The tikoloshe delighted, observing her follower take pleasure in the consumption of human spirit. For Soepenberg no longer suffered the dissatisfaction of the human condition, in death he became a new breed of creature, no longer consigned by restraints which you and I are held to in our daily humdrum lives, his mind and body set free to roam the savannah between life and death, a dimension of existence we all eventually encounter yet from which few return.

Ascending on the ecstasy of assimilating Arnou's spirit, he became aware of the course his life was to flow.

"Yes, you see it," whispered the tikoloshe.
Soepenberg recoiled from his high returning to the land of the living, soul revitalised, yet he understood it would diminish over time unless replenished.
"Yes, this is the curse of eternal life, you must feed upon the living," instructed the wizened witch.
Soepenberg peered at a crackling crone rested behind the fire, "Eternal life? What of my wife? Where does she dwell in this eternity?" inquired the blonde beast in Afrikaans.
The wrinkled sangoma cackled, "A rare dessert, her soul was truly glorious."
The Afrikaner retrieved Arnou's dagger, its tip pointed toward the tikoloshe in fateful fury, the white demon spat his following sentence as a man might reject rotten curry, "You devoured my Hannah?"
"Calm yourself apprentice," snapped the tikoloshe, somewhat annoyed by his actions, "it was not I who condemned her to death nor did I murder her, you have already taken revenge upon that one."
"But you consumed Hannah?"
"Rein yourself in apprentice, the demon in you must be controlled. It is powerful yet may be pacified, provided you feed it the souls of men."
"What if I consume your soul?" he moved around dying embers until nothing prevented Soepenberg from taking the old crone in his hands and breaking her neck, just as he'd done moments ago with Arnou.
The crone didn't move from her crouched stance, she merely smiled while drawing a bone from within her leather belt.

Pointing the bone at Soepenberg he felt intense pain hit his body, curiously it was at the area indicated by the tikoloshe's cartilage.

The white rat dropped his dagger immediately, its blade disappearing inside a combination of gloom and dust.

The evil spirit cackled as a strike of demonic lightning forked into the white man's body. An evil Afrikaner risen from the dead to serve a malevolence as dark as Africa and ancient as the pharaohs.

Lightening forked, then, forked again and again and again, bringing the Afrikaner to his knees until he rested at eye level with a wrinkled tikoloshe, cackling in delight she dined on his pain, a succulent appetizer in a demonic banquet.

Soepenberg screamed, alerting all those in Kokstad for his cry did resemble a possessed wild dog bellowing over African plains, terrifying all of God's creatures for miles around.

The Khoi-san quarter began to empty as grown men, minds and bodies chiselled as an impi warrior in his prime, fled for their lives. Xhosa followed as satanic roars rocked their accommodations, shaking straw from hut roofs to mud foundations.

A great stampede of human beings rushed through Kokstad as a bad case of diarrhoea, combined with the diabolical noise of a demonic creature convulsing atmosphere, all had been alerted to an evil presence inhabiting Kokstad and none were prepared to confront it, save one man.

The tikoloshe's attention was drawn away from its vile banquet. Despite the succulent sensation of biting a hunk from Soepenberg's spirit it withdrew.

Soepenberg dropped, face down into dark dust lining the sangoma's hut, panting for his life as a whipped dog begging its master for mercy.

"Leave," stated the tikoloshe with urgency, "quickly, for the white lion draws near."

For reasons unclear the tikoloshe was uneasy at the thought of sharing the same space with the white lion.

"Take this," the creature took a bag of gold coin from beneath its belt and held it out, yet Soepenberg remained face down collecting his consciousness before attempting to stand.

For the first time the tikoloshe displayed outright anger, its voice deepened, a noise similar to African war drums beating in the night, their direction obscure yet they became louder and louder, moving in on the listener's position, "Dispose of the San and leave this place."

Soepenberg pulled his face from the dirt, took the demon's offering of coin and began to lift Arnou's corpse from the floor, "What must I do?"

"Go east then north, satisfy your hunger and take revenge on those who wished me banished from Kokstad," replied the tikoloshe.

Soepenberg lifted Arnou's limp cadaver from dirt floor, slinging it over his shoulder he exited through sheeted gateway into desolate slum, devoid of human habitation. After disposing slaughtered San into a drainage ditch, the white rat made his way into town where he might purchase supplies for his coming journey.

A fresh horse, food and water, a map, he outfitted himself before moving north through Zululand and into the Transvaal region where the tikoloshe's enemies lay, there he would engage in the most vile and villainous trade, that of human flesh, while satisfying his hunger for a brand of African spirit not found within glass bottle but vessel of flesh and bone.

At the livery the blonde Boer scanned equine beasts, as he passed close several horses became wary, neighing in fear and terror.

The proprietor approached from behind, "I don't know what's got into 'em today," stated a tall Griqua, shirt rolled up to his elbows, a pair of tough denim trousers. Denim being a French fabric known as "serge de Nimes" the "de Nimes" eventually becoming the English word "denim"; he also wore a pair of tough leather boots and a leather outback hat.

Soepenberg pointed at a jet black stallion in the far corner, it silently eyed the pair of humans as they scrutinized chaos caused by the shoving and neighing of other beasts, "That one."

The stableman chuckled, "Nah, you don't want 'im, he's a right terror. Save yourself the backache mate, one bloke was laid up for two weeks after he threw 'im."

Soepenberg was insistent, "I want that one."

The stableman sighed, "Alrighty then, but don't expect me to pay when he chucks you ... they don't call 'im Diablo for nothing!"

The dastardly Dutchman walked through the stable towards Diablo, yet the stableman witnessed a very odd occurrence, for as Soepenberg approached the dark steed, other stallions separated, opening a path to the black beast. Diablo, unlike other steeds in the stable, remained absolutely calm.

Upon reaching Diablo the stableman expected a violent reaction, yet the creature remained compliant, in fact when the Afrikaner presented fresh fodder it ate from his hand before being led from the stable.

Looking the stable master in the eye he said, "How much?"

The Griqua scratched his head, "Well I never! I usually let my stock go for a guinea but considering the amount of bloody trouble this one's cost me, I'll let you have him for ten bob."

The stable master used British money since other denominations circulating at this time were only good for local use and he could always change British money into any local currency he wished since it was trusted the world over.

Soepenberg produced a purse given to him by the tikoloshe, immediately the stable master recognised the sangoma's mark and interjected before money changed hands, "Never mind mate, you take 'im."

The Griqua would rather donate Diablo than taint his hands with blood money, possibly cursing his family for generations.

"Are you sure?" inquired Soepenberg.

"Aye, I'm sure."

As a black stallion trotted out of town it passed a pair of British officers, their pith helmets tall and brass badges bright in hot African sun.

"Sir?" stated Wood in an incredulous tone.

"I see him," replied Chelmsford, his vision befuddled by an image of Soepenberg exiting town on horseback, unblemished by their previous encounter.

The blonde Boer left town in the direction of his farm, not to re-establish his residency but recover goods necessary to his future trade, slavery.

He'd retrieve basic clothing, equipment for Diablo and most importantly his treasured blunderbuss.

"Sir, how in blue blazes do you explain that?" remarked the Colonel as he scrutinized the Boer's back; for despite wearing a fresh shirt it would certainly fail to hold back bloody lacerations inflicted via British frontier justice.

"I cannot, nevertheless, hitherto it's time we leave this place, set task has been consummated and I'm obliged to send the High Commissioner a report immediately."

"Yes Sir, do you wish to telegraph Cape Town our success?" said Wood as he stood to attention.

"That would be proper, and while you're at it request the High Commissioner's direction concerning his letter to Kreli," replied an upright General with foreboding tone.

Said letter was a declaration of war to be delivered to the Chief of Gcalekaland, or at least it's most powerful chief and paramount house of the Xhosa nation, King Ka Hintsa Sarhili, otherwise known as Chief Kreli.

The ninth and final Xhosa war was to commence after a group of Gcaleka ambushed a predominantly Fengu militia while policing Cape Town. The incident far less grand than described in official dispatches, for it stemmed from a bar brawl during wedding celebrations in Cape Town and when African beer, that is umqombothi, collides with tribal resentment the Devil is unleashed. It was the perfect pre-text to invasion, added to that the attempt by Griquas to kidnap his niece lent license to shape the fate of two nations.

First Griqualand East was to be offered protectorate status, for they had no military with which to resist; once established Frederic would push north east into the Xhosa Kingdom to deliver a second set of cruel correspondence, surrender or war.

The British were moving in on Xhosa territory in what would be a two year war, ending in Kreli's capture not far from Zululand where the lion and rat would collide once again.

The End

Printed in Great Britain
by Amazon

38508154R10131